# Struck

## Origin of Love Book 1

### Fallen Immortals Saga

♦

## Jendela Tryst

# Struck: Origin of Love Book 1

Copyright © 2014 by Converging Horizons

Published by Converging Horizons Publishing
www.converginghorizons.com

First Edition

ISBN-13: 978-1499705362
ISBN-10: 1499705360

Library of Congress Control Number: 2015936125

For "Magistra" Kathryn Jarvis

1948-2006

Ambulatio memoranda.

# Greek Gods and Goddesses

Aphrodite - Goddess of love, beauty, procreation, pleasure

Apollo - God of the sun, healing, prophesy

Ares - God of war, bloodshed, violence

Artemis - Goddess of the moon, virginity, hunting

Athena - Goddess of wisdom, war, battle strategy

Demeter - Goddess of grain, agriculture, harvest

Dionysus - God of wine, parties, ecstasy

Eros - God of love and passion

Hades - God of the underworld and the dead

Hephaestus - Gitod of metalwork, fire, crafts

Hera - Queen of the gods, marriage, childbirth

Hermes – God of language, writing, theivery diplomacy, athletics

Poseidon - God of the sea, rivers, floods

Zeus - King of the Gods, lightning, law, order, fate

# Prologue

Apollo, god of the sun, stood at the threshold of Aphrodite's palace, holding a thin laurel tree branch that he gripped like a sword ready for attack. Aphrodite, goddess of beauty, gazed upon him calmly, reaching to her left for another plump, purple fig which she bit into slowly, her lush, pink lips and youthful cheeks defying the agedness of her glacial blue eyes.

"Where is he?" Apollo's voice boomed through the elaborate corridors, causing the reliefs on the Corsican columns to tremble in fright.

"Where is who, dear brother?" Aphrodite's melodious, feminine and effortlessly seductive voice was a sharp contrast to his.

"That addlepated twit you call a son!"

There was a flicker of interest in her eyes and she paused in her chewing. "Eros? Why, I have not seen him all day."

"You lie! I know he's hiding in here somewhere, cowering behind your skirts like the gutless mongrel that he is."

Apollo raised his voice and shook the branch at the ceiling. "You hear that, Eros, you demi-god of riffraff and all that's unholy! You are naught but a little craven! A spineless, useless miscreant!"

"Please lower your voice. You'll disturb my peacocks that are resting in the gardens."

"To Tartarus with your peacocks!"

"Oh really, Apollo, you're starting to give me a headache. Could you at least explain what all the ruckus is about? Did he try to steal your phaeton again? Or did he lure away one of your water nymphs from your grasp? Perhaps if you had a more delicate touch they wouldn't fly away so quickly."

Apollo's response was a withering glare that sent one of Aphrodite's winged servants flapping away in fright. Aphrodite, however, remained unmoved.

"She did not give me the chance to touch her."

He looked at the brown branch in his hand with pained eyes. It only had a few bruised leaves left hanging from the ends.

"A wood nymph. Daphne. He all but destroyed her. It is all his fault that she is lost to me forever!"

"Well unless he seduced her himself, I don't see how that could be possible."

"Do you not?" He shook the pathetic tree limb at her. "You're the one who gifted him those blasted arrows!"

"Oh, pah! Eros's arrows cannot affect the gods. Love in that obsessive form is a purely human thing. You don't mean to say that you, Apollo the noble, god of light and the sun, truth, prophecy, medicine, healing, archery, music, poetry, arts and sport, was affected by a child's plaything?"

Conflicting feelings warred in Apollo's eyes as he thought of the implications of Aphrodite's comment. He shook his head as if it hurt, his voice softening slightly. "Eros is no longer a child. And..."

"And what?" She said coyly.

"And his damn arrows are getting more and more powerful!" All softness vanished from his angry voice.

"Is that so? Because I don't hear of anyone else complaining. Is it truly the arrows that are getting more powerful, dear brother, or are you starting to be more prone to... weaknesses?"

"Eh?"

Aphrodite observed the evenness of her fingernails as she continued.

"Perhaps you are getting a little too old for your work now, dragging that gargantuan chariot across the world day in and day out along with that hot, ill-tempered sun. You must be quite exhausted. Perhaps it's time you retired, settle down with a proper immortal wife and make lots of sunny little babies."

"And who, pray, do you envision taking over my godly duties?"

"Eros has a strong arm with a phaeton. His phoenix is the fastest in all of Olympus. As for his archery skills, well, you can attest to that. He never misses his target, man or immortal, no matter how fast."

"Hah! I would rather die a thousand deaths and be married to Hades himself!" Apollo spat on the immaculate marble floors. "I see what you're getting at, little sister. And if you think I will ever give

6

up my duties as god of light and truth, much less give it to that ne'er-do-well lying piece of toad spittle, you are very much mistaken. I don't know what you've done with Eros's arrows, but I will be watching him very carefully. One of these days, he's going to slip up. And I will be the first to make sure he stays down."

"Ugh, brother, you look so ugly with your brows furrowed thus. Please begone from my sight or you will give me frown wrinkles too."

"Zeus forbid your beauty ever fades, Aphrodite. That is all you have to boast of, everyone knows brains are not your strength. But get this. There is already talk down in the grape valley of a maiden more lovely, even than you. Perhaps she could take over your duties, being that your rank has been surpassed."

At last, a flash of true anger crossed Aphrodite's celestial eyes. "Hah, what foolishness is this?"

"I'm surprised you have not heard. The mortals speak of nothing else these days besides the war between Troy and Greece, of course. She has apparently served as a lovely distraction. They say that had she been among those competing for Paris's Golden Apples, the prize for being the fairest in all the world, she would have plucked it right out of your greedy little hands."

Anger was turning the natural pink blush of Aphrodite's cheeks a deeper, more crimson red. However, this only enhanced her charming beauty. "What is this? A mortal? A mortal woman more beautiful than I?"

"Aye, and more intelligent, honorable, and virtuous than you as well. Hah, but that is not much of a task, is it? Perhaps if you stopped staring at your own reflection so much, you might be aware of the great offense."

"Enough!" She flicked her delicate wrist in his direction. "You have gotten away with abusing my son in my very own home, you will not be allowed to say such things to me! Begone from here and take that daft branch with you. It's dropping leaves all over my floor."

"This daft branch is from a tree that was once the most beloved nymph in all the land! All because of your wretched son! You and everyone else will honor it!"

Without another word, Apollo stormed out, taking his sad, shedding twig with him.

The moment he left, Aphrodite rose with a speed that belied her previously lethargic position. Immediately, she moved to a shimmering fountain and gazed at her reflection. A frown was marring her beauty and a curl had fallen out of place. She replaced the golden ringlet immediately in to its proper position and sat touching the water. Her mood lightened as she gazed upon her stunning reflection. She touched the water lovingly.

*More beautiful than I?* She chuckled at the ridiculous notion.

"Show me this maiden who is said to be more beautiful than the winner of the Golden Apples, the most beautiful goddess in Olympus, I, goddess of exquisiteness, passionate love, and sensuous pleasure," she commanded, smiling as her image continued to gaze back at her. For a while, it continued to reflect her divine face unwaveringly. Aphrodite began thinking of all the ways she would punish Apollo for his little lies.

Then, slowly, another face began to replace her own, blurring in the frothing water.

At first, Aphrodite did not look impressed, but the longer she stared and the clearer the vision came, the deeper the lines of displeasure marred her face. She leaned forward, picking up on the small details of the young lady reflected in the water. The goddess's face grew darker with every passing moment. Finally, she gave a sharp cry and summoned her owl who swooped from a pedestal and landed on a meticulous finger that she extended for the bird.

"I want you to look for Eros. I need him here immediately!"

The snowy white owl nodded its consent and immediately flew through an open window. As it flapped away bidding the wind to carry him faster, the owl could hear the angry bellow of its mistress.

"How dare she!"

The owl's feathers ruffled and he flapped more vigorously. He'd hate to be the object of Aphrodite's rage.

# Chapter 1

Lucius, the horse trader, frowned at the ominous gray clouds that curled just above the hilltops beyond the rows of grape vines recently plucked bare of ripe fruit. His companion, Marcus, to whom the vineyard belonged, was adjusting the straps of his sandals and missed the frown that marred the young man's bearded mouth.

"Apollo is in a sad state this evening," Lucius murmured under his breath.

Marcus looked up and followed his gaze. "Just a bit of rain, Lucius. No need for superstition."

Lucius did not change his solemn countenance. "Call it what you will, but the weather is quite appropriate for the occasion. The end of harvest is often full of debauchery and sacrilege."

"Do you mean the tavern over yonder forest? Really, I don't see what's wrong with a little wine and brew now and then. In fact, I was just heading over there myself as long as our business is finished here. You are free to join me if you like."

"No, not I. I am heading over to visit with Master Halsted. His youngest daughter has recently returned from a visit with her sister and I am eager to see her again."

"Young Psyche is back, is she? She'd been gone for quite a while, I'd say."

"Almost a year," Lucius answered almost too quickly.

"I shall have to pay my respects when I get the chance. She was quite a clever little one. Unfortunate that she is so uncomely."

"You have not heard? She has been quite transformed, they say."

"I can't imagine how such a transformation can occur. I remember her as being a boyish, stick of a thing. Nothing to her older sisters who were clearly kissed by Aphrodite."

Lucius's reserved smile was non-committing. "This is true, but she did have a strong mind, for a woman," Lucius continued earnestly, "and an intriguing perspective. It would be nice if she could square away a little debate her father and I had the other week."

"Debating with that old scholar again? I don't know why you even bother, Lucius. He is so clever he could outwit Hermes himself!"

Lucius frowned again, causing Marcus to shift uncomfortably. Lucius was an honest tradesman, for that he was grateful for one was certain to get a fair price for a solid workhorse. But it didn't mean that he liked Lucius's constant disapproval for the most harmless phrases. He would be grateful to take his leave and be among his friends again, men who knew how to laugh and be merry.

Marcus cleared his throat. "Well then, I should not keep you here and our old friend waiting. Give my regards to Master Halsted and his homely daughter."

"I shall. Good day to you, Marcus."

The two men grasped opposite arms just below the elbows and parted ways respectfully.

Unbeknownst to the two men, a cloaked figure crouched, hiding in the shadows of the gnarled tree branches high above their heads, watching the men extend their distance. He leaned fearless among the trees, as if the branches were a hammock and death did not daunt him. He observed the pair of mortals with bemused interest. A part of him was interested in following the yellow haired one with the beard simply for the pleasure of meeting the old scholar who was so clever, he might actually be able to outwit him, Hermes, the god of trickery himself. And the uncomely daughter with a strong mind was sure to amuse him. But alas, Hermes was in this little village of Bromeia for another purpose and a crowded alehouse was the perfect place for a meeting.

With some reluctance, the god headed in the direction of the dark-haired one who was whistling as he trotted his newly purchased horse up a well-travelled road. With a flash of his winged heels, Hermes flew well past the farmer towards the debauched and sacrilegious house of ale.

Marcus smiled as he entered the noisy tavern. It was the end of a grueling harvest day and the workers crushed to get their fill of drink. The smell of unwashed sweat and skin wafted through the room, but nobody seemed to mind it, greeting old friends and catching up with village gossip.

There was one person not exchanging pleasantries. He was a strange man who sat alone at a corner table, his face covered in a commoner's brown woolen hood, blending with his surroundings and half vanishing in the shadows. Although the place was crowded, there was a distinct space between him and the others, and the only empty stool was in front of him, even as men stood and crushed together wishing for a seat.

Marcus, feeling weary from the long day, moved to take the empty stool. A tug of it revealed that it was stuck. He tried again, and still it wouldn't move. He looked down and saw that the stranger's ankle was effortlessly holding the leg of the stool in place.

"This seat is taken," came a low, articulate voice from under the hood.

Though the hooded man appeared much slighter than the bulky farmer, there was something in his tone that made Marcus think twice about arguing. Instead, he muttered agitatedly under his breath, then turned to take a seat from someone else.

An almost imperceptible breeze blew gently through the open door and a handful of men nearby turned curiously to see who had entered. Some gasped with pleasure. Others looked away disapprovingly. A woman appeared in men's hunting clothes. Despite her attire, she strode in with a warrior's swagger, carrying on her curved, womanly hips, a sheathed short sword while strapped to her back was a fierce-looking spear. After pausing briefly to scan the room with sharp eyes, she headed to the corner where the hooded man sat.

"Not very subtle, Athena." The murmur uttered out in an unfamiliar language from the hooded figure. No one nearby could decipher it despite their curiosity.

"I do not believe in disguises," she replied airily. Her voice was like a cool northerly wind, deep and husky. "You know it is against my nature. You are lucky I did away with my armor completely."

"Would you rather appear in all your radiant glory and have the entire place screaming in terror?"

She replied with a twinkle in her eye, "It would give us a quieter place to talk."

"Noise is the only thing that prevents others from hearing us. You don't want all the gods to know our secrets, do you?"

She shrugged and pointed to his hooded attire. "You have certainly found a suitable enough disguise, Hermes."

"Thank you." He played at his hood.

"The god of trickery blends well with criminals and thieves. The look suits you more than you'll ever know."

The hood shook imperceptibly, but it wasn't in anger, which the unknowing eye may have guessed, but with rich laughter. Hermes loved a good insult.

"These aren't criminals," he protested playfully. "These are hard working men of agriculture! Furthermore, I am not just a god of trickery. I am also the god of poetry and music."

"And I'm Zeus's legitimate daughter," came the sarcastic retort.

Athena, illegitimate daughter of Zeus, king of the gods, was given much honor in Olympus, being the goddess of war and wisdom, admired as well as feared. Hera, Queen of the gods and Zeus's wife, was far from pleased with the arrangement.

"Your illegitimacy is a secret blessing," Hermes assured her. "Heavens forbid, you have an ounce of Hera in your blood."

Athena smiled briefly. "But I haven't time to dally, Hermes. I need your message."

"Not even a drink for old time's sake?" He smiled.

The goddess hesitated, staring into the charm of the young god's dark eyes beneath the hood. "Very well, one drink only. Although this really is not a good time for me."

Hermes dreaded bringing up the dark subject that always managed to put everyone in a foul mood, but he sensed Athena needed to vent.

"How is Troy?"

"Utter chaos. No one is listening to anyone. It is as if complete self-annihilation will be the only solution."

"Something must be done."

"All of Olympus is divided on the matter. We are as much at war with each other as the Greeks are with Troy! I am quite exhausted." Athena sighed.

"You favor Greece, of course."

"But of course! If that Paris hadn't taken what wasn't his, this would never have happened! And if that damned Aphrodite hadn't given that girl to him without the slightest consideration of the impact, well, we wouldn't be having this conversation, would we? That sorry excuse for a goddess cares about nothing but herself."

Hermes smiled a secret smile. Although there was some truth to Athena's declarations, he also knew that the goddess was still smarting from Paris's epic snub. A Trojan prince, Paris had been given the task of judging who was the most beautiful of the three goddesses, Hera, Athena, or Aphrodite. As with many competitions between the gods, bribery was necessary for a final decision. Hera, goddess of all the gods, promised Paris wealth beyond imagination. Athena, believing she knew the heart of man best, promised him power and military might. Then Aphrodite searched deep into his soul and offered him the most beautiful woman in the world. For Paris, there was no competition. He already loved the most beautiful woman in world. Known as Helen of Troy, she was already married to the King of Sparta, Menelaus. When Aphrodite was chosen as fairest, she had no choice but to give Paris his promised lady, so Paris and Helen ran away together, back to the protection of Troy. Menelaus, enraged by Helen's abandonment, demanded her return. When Troy denied him, a great war resulted, tearing the entire Aegean sea and Mount Olympus, home of the gods, as the immortals bickered over who should win victory.

"I cannot fathom why all of you care so much about human wars." Hermes shook his head.

"Not all of us can have your dispassionate neutrality, brother," Athena responded. "Some of us are capable of picking sides and remaining loyal."

"What use is loyalty when all it causes is grief? Neutrality is the only tolerable path. I cannot even remember when Olympus was at peace with each other."

"I remember." The goddess's eyes softened at the memory. "The wedding, of course."

"Ah yes!" Hermes smiled, remembering the dancing and the wine, and of course the music. Oh, the music! "A more unlikely match I couldn't have imagined."

"Hades and Persephone. How could such a thing have happened?"

"I can make a guess." This was a much more pleasant topic! Athena, having gotten her drink at last, was beginning to relax. The wedding of Hades, god of death and the underworld, and Persephone, daughter of the earth goddess, had been such a surprise. Hades was the only god dressed in macabre black, but his smiling teeth did reveal a white joy rarely witnessed even after hundreds of years of acquaintance. Why, the sallow fellow almost looked handsome in the sunlight! Surprises rarely happened in the world of the gods, only when another god manipulated something.

"Eros?" Athena read his mind.

"Of course."

"I cannot imagine that little boy having anything to do with something so elaborate— so brilliant in fact."

"We are always underestimating him. And he is no longer a little boy. He has grown much over the years."

Athena chortled. "Underestimate him and his harmless little arrows? Really, Hermes, you give that scoundrel too much credit. They have never once affected me."

"Never?" Hermes's eyes bored into hers and Athena found herself unable to hold his gaze. Sensing she did not want to talk about a particular incident that involved a young man many years ago, Hermes shrugged nonchalantly, releasing her from his stare. "Well, Eros's arrows are supposed to be more potent on men."

"I cannot imagine them working on a squirrel!" his vigilant companion snapped. She surprised him by continuing stiffly. "I admit there was an incident, long ago when I was still a naive young goddess, where a youth may have... affected me. But that was not because of Eros! The young man in question was very... exceptional." Her eyes clouded at the memory, a disturbing sight for Hermes who wasn't used to seeing Athena showing any weakness. "Never mind." She shook her head slightly as if it hurt. "He is gone now, and he had nothing to do with Eros. We are all better off."

Athena was too honorable to lie so Hermes could see that she was convinced of this. Hermes marveled at her ability for self-deceit. The young man she spoke of was not merely gone, he was killed by Athena herself, who knew that to have him would be impossible and to not have him, to allow another to have him, even more so. In a way, it had been a choice between her ordained place as Athena, the goddess of war and wisdom, and Athena, mother and wife. Clearly she chose her godly duties. It was what made her a goddess. The scars of that choice, however, were clearly greater than any inflicted by battle.

Athena had never loved another.

"Well, even if that were true, Eros does have a powerful affect on some men. Love is a powerful motivator."

"He is his mother's child," Athena's tone suggested she thought little of this connection. "He hasn't a thought that's not full of beautiful females that bloat up his vanity. Whatever work he does, it is because that whimsical mother demands it of him. He hasn't a mind of his own."

Before Hermes could respond, a male voice sounded from above their heads.

"Who needs a mind when you have a heart?"

Hermes and Athena looked up to see Eros in human form looking as devastatingly handsome as Athena was beautiful, perhaps more so.

If their new arrival had heard most of the conversation, he did not reveal it.

His smile was all teeth, perfect in its straightness and symmetry, his blue eyes were two dancing blue jays between long, wheat colored lashes. He was dressed as a sheepherder, complete with a dusty streak across his cheek that only accentuated the perfect, manly slopes of his face and the charming, youthful indentation of his dimples. Hermes would have given his wings to

15

have a face like Eros. Although he was no bane on the eyes himself, the messenger god looked like a haggard beggar next to the smiling god of love.

# Chapter 2

"Ah, look. It is our little nephew, all heart and very little mind." Athena's smile widened across her cheeks.

"We are so happy to see you," Hermes chimed in. "What brings you here, my lad? But hold, let me get you a seat." He tapped a huge man who had his back towards him on the shoulder. Marcus, Hermes had heard his friends call him.

The man turned, his face dangerously dark with annoyance, but Hermes did not seem to notice. "I'd like your chair."

Farmer Marcus's thunderous look would have sent a mortal man fleeing in fright, but after peering into the hood, Marcus stopped. No one in the room knew what he saw, but the farmer suddenly unclenched his fist and moved slightly back. Hermes, as if realizing that he was causing a small scene, softened his voice and added a curt, "Please."

Instantly, Marcus gave up the seat.

Before Eros sat down, he patted the burly man's shoulder amicably. "So good of you, kind sir!"

The comment relieved the tension and everyone looked away from the exchange. The god of love then turned his smiling, dazzling face back to Hermes.

"What on earth are you doing here, lad?" Hermes dropped his hood and leaned forward. "This is the last place I would have expected you."

"The Fates must be drunk again," Eros replied soberly.

Hermes paused in confusion. He saw the glint in Eros's eyes, then both men began laughing, picturing the ancient, toothless, oh-so-pious Fates drunk and slovenly.

Athena remained unmoved, clearly irritated by the intrusion, never mind the blasphemy. The holy and sacred Fates should never be mocked in such a way!

Eros leaned back on his chair, stretching out his legs. "I am here on an errand. Not the most pleasant, I'm afraid, so I figured I'd procrastinate a bit at this jolly little alehouse. Also, I had a feeling I might run into a few friends. Just a hunch, of course." It was no secret that the immortals of Olympus could sense one another when they were near.

"And what is this unpleasant errand, young Eros?" Hermes asked amicably, "Is it something we may assist you with?"

"Hermes may assist you," Athena cut in. "I have more important things to do,"

Both gods cheerfully ignored her. "Although I appreciate the offer, it is not something that I can't handle myself. It's really quite beneath me, but alas, mother would trust no other with the task."

This seemed to capture Athena's attention. "What could possibly be so beneath you, Eros?" Athena dug in. Hermes' mouth twitched at the clever insult, but he did not laugh.

A shadow finally crossed Eros's otherwise cheerful disposition, but he controlled his irritation, if it had been that. "I am to torture a beautiful woman who claims to be more beautiful than all the goddesses, including my mother."

Athena rolled her eyes and took another sip of ale. "Oh, how typical of Ditty. To get so caught up in something so trivial."

"You would know much about triviality, Athena. My mother's Golden Apples hang quite decorously on her mantle. You should come by to see it sometime."

The Golden Apples were the prize for having been chosen by Paris as the most beautiful goddess. It had been a slight on Athena's beauty, and was clearly still a sore spot for Athena.

Hermes interrupted before Athena could react. Baiting the goddess of war was never a good idea. Both had it coming, but hand-to-hand combat between gods could completely wipe out the entire alehouse. Perhaps even the entire city. Hermes knew from experience. "Who is this young woman?"

"Oh, I have no idea. I have not found her yet. I was hoping the locals could reveal to me where she lived."

"Truly, nephew," Athena adjusted her armband. "To have to rely on locals for such things. It must kill you not to have the All-Seeing Eye."

"Not at all. Such things should be reserved for the most powerful of gods, even when they are not the prettiest.

Athena hissed, but before she could respond, Hermes touched her hand.

"He means no harm, Athena," Hermes injected. "We all know the competition was rigged from the beginning."

As Athena toyed with her drink, she regained her composure and managed to smile stiffly. "It is good that you remind us of your limitations, little Eros. Hermes was just trying to convince me that you had something to do with Hades finding that unfortunate Persephone for a queen. I told him that there was no way a god so small and weak could affect such a mighty being like the great Hades, god of the Underworld, superseded in power only by Zeus himself."

Hermes watched Eros carefully. If the robin's eggs in his eyes moved a little less merrily, it was only a minute change. But, Hermes was acute for a reason. Athena did not have this gift and she never would. It was why she always demanded the truth. She did not want to exert herself differentiating a lie.

Eros's voice was defeated. "Alas, you are right on this point, Athena. Hermes thinks a little too highly of me. My arrows cannot affect the gods."

Hermes's eyes narrowed. It was a smooth lie, but it was a lie, he was certain of it. He was beginning to suspect Eros was more powerful than even he realized. Perhaps, not even Zeus was immune to Eros's arrows. To have the power to affect Zeus was a dangerous ability. A highly forbidden and punishable ability.

Athena, bored with the discussion, pushed her seat back. "Well, it is as I thought. Now, I must go. Unlike some people in this room, I have very important work to do. I have men dying by the thousands. My temples are overcrowded with wives and kinsman begging for my blessings. On both sides."

"You must not keep them waiting," Hermes smiled graciously and stood up. "But before you go…" he leaned forward and whispered a message to Athena's ears.

Eros watched curiously as Athena's eyes became troubled. She looked back at Hermes, her voice not as soft as his. "A wooden horse…. Most… unusual. Not the way I would have preferred it done. Not very honorable, I should say."

Hermes sighed and took another sip ale. "I have already visited the Greek commander, Achilles's dream. It is to be started upon tomorrow."

Athena's frown deepened, but she took a deep breath. "Well, if that is what Zeus wishes... I just hoped..." Something shifted in Athena's mind, and instantly, the hesitation vanished and her eyes cleared. "Never mind, it is not in my hands. I'm sure Zeus has his reasons. If that is the only way, then so it must be. Hermes, I am glad to see you are well. I don't admire what you're doing, not taking sides, but I understand you are merely Zeus's messenger and must remain neutral."

"Thank you for your understanding, sister. Neutrality is also a way to keep one's sanity."

"A little insanity never hurt anyone," Eros chimed.

Athena sniffed. "Loyalty, righteousness, honor, these are not forms of insanity and should never be thought of as such." She nodded briefly at her nephew in a barely cordial farewell, "Eros."

"Athena," he said more reverently with a bow.

To Hermes, Athena's smile was broader, revealing rare warmth that Eros envied. The goddess of war extended her arm which Hermes grasped at the elbow.

When the goddess breezed past them, Eros breathed a sigh of relief and relaxed more comfortably in his seat. "I do not know what I ever did to that one!"

"You were born to a mother she hates, my boy. Forget her. Please take a seat closer! It has been ages."

Before Eros sat down on the chair Athena just vacated, he turned to the hulking figure standing next to him. "You, man," he tapped boldly on the back of the burly farmer. "You may have your borrowed chair back. We thank you graciously for it."

The man turned, surprised at the friendly warmth in Eros's eyes, then grunted and sat down.

"That is a very fine man!" Eros declared. "I am going to make sure he gets a good wife one day."

Hermes scanned the man's head and shoulders briefly, reading his thoughts. Marcus was a farmer and his wife was the frigid sort, which was probably why he kept staring at a buxom, smiling serving girl with longing in his eyes. "I believe he is already married," Hermes cast him an accusing look. "To a bit of a termagant if I may say."

"Is that so? Well, I had nothing to do with it."

"You probably had everything to do with it. You are the god of love."

"People marry for other reasons. If they do, it is hardly my fault. Perhaps I'll give him a lovely young mistress to boost his spirits."

"I do not believe him giving up a chair warrants such a generous reward."

"Alas, if you say so."

Eros's humility was not of this world and Hermes leaned in impatiently. "You know, I like to think I'm a pretty clever fellow, but I don't quite know you as well as I would like."

"How so? We've known each other almost all our lives." Eros was focusing on the thread that was poking out of his sleeve. When he saw the attractive serving lady nearby, he called out, "Mistress! More ale this way. Two, please!"

"Oh, I am fine," Hermes protested, pointing to his still partially full cup.

"No, uncle, they are for me." His smile was dazzling. "This garb looks truly authentic, does it not? I completely imitated the likeness of a young shepherd I saw on my way over here. It is dirty and unkempt, but quite comfortable, especially the shoes." For emphasis, he lifted his foot and revealed ragged kidskins.

Hermes nodded at the handsome toes poking out of the sandals and opted for a more direct approach, one that could not lead to deliberate misinterpretation. "What do you have to gain from making Hades so happy? There is no reward in it for you. He does not know what you have done so he will never return the favor. What is the reason for such an act of generosity?"

"I honestly haven't the slightest clue what you are talking about, my dear uncle," Eros persevered and smiled a guileless smile. "But I am flattered, truly flattered by the high honor you insist on giving me. If only I had such power." There was a brief pause when Eros suddenly lowered his voice slightly. "As for the happiness of

21

Hades, had I had the strength or the inclination to grant it—which I don't, mind you!—then, why wouldn't I? He is not a hateful man, that Hades. He is a dutiful worker. Never takes a holiday. Furthermore, he may just be the most just of all the gods, for based on what I hear, after a mortal dies, his judgment is quite unbiased. He cannot be bribed or cajoled. The wicked go to hell and the good find eternal happiness, and that is nothing to scoff at. Sometimes I wish Earth could be ruled with such justice."

"You do have a point there, lad. Hades deserves happiness like any other. Just because he is taciturn and morbid, cannot laugh at a joke or even make a joke if his life depended on it, does not make him evil."

"Unless it is a sin to be a terrible bore."

Hermes considered this. "I often tell Zeus it ought to be."

"Hell would be far too overcrowded," Eros pointed out.

"But much more repugnant!" Smiling, Hermes realized he had been swayed from the subject again. He shook his head and took a long sip of ale, bidding himself to stay focused.

Not to be bested in his own game, Hermes returned to the subject at hand. "But poor Demeter, Persephone's mother. Did you not think about her sadness to lose her daughter to the god of the Underworld?"

"I had naught to do with either. If I get no credit for Hades' happiness, why should I get blame for Demeter's sadness?" His eyes did not meet his uncle, but his nonchalant shrug could have fooled a lesser god. Hermes knew it was time to let this one go. Eros was not about to give in, and Hermes would have to find the true reason behind it. Fear perhaps? Or simply unwanted glory? Hermes did not know anyone, god or man, who did not revel in glory. He realized he knew his nephew much less than he had thought.

"Of course," Hermes conceded. "You are as innocent as a lamb."

Eros rose, making courteous excuses. Hermes had scared him off. Perhaps it was best. Hermes did not know what he would do with the truth of Eros's power if confirmed. Report it to Zeus, perhaps? That was the dutiful answer. Or should he remain neutral and let the Fates determine the outcome?

Hermes rose cordially. "Before you leave, my dear Eros, remember this: In trying to grant everyone happiness, do not neglect your own."

"Ah, but that is already accomplished. There is not a morning I see the sun rise that I do not find myself the happiest god alive!"

Another lie, Hermes sighed, but he appreciated the rhyme. Rhymes always made Hermes happy. He was surprised to see a heavy arm grasp his shoulder and suddenly Eros was next to him looking earnest, his eyes were soft, gentle pools.

"You are a good friend, Hermes."

Hermes covered the hand briefly with his.

He watched as Eros melted away into the crowd politely pushing his way through. There was a sudden jolt, then the sound of a chair falling, and Hermes heard his nephew apologize gently to the buxom young serving woman who had bumped into him. Surprised by his beautiful manners, she stumbled again and landed right in farmer Marcus's brawny arms. Her face was crimson as she lay on his lap and struggled to get up.

"Why, hello there," said the farmer with a toothy grin, and she began to giggle like a child.

Hermes looked up only to see that his young friend had disappeared. He shook his head and drank the last of his ale before dropping coins down on the table. It was going to be a busy evening. There were several dreams he had to visit and the messages he had to give were not pleasing. Hopefully, Eros would do his job well in spreading love this night. For Hermes, his job was to spread a much darker, fearful emotion.

Eros breathed in the night air. That had been a difficult interview. It would have been good to confess to Hermes the torment and regret he was feeling over what he had done. By matching Persephone with Hades, he had denied Demeter, a devoted mother, the happiness of spending her life with her daughter by her side.

Sometimes his meddling only caused more trouble. Every time Eros tried to do good, something bad negated all his work.

But, Hermes was not the best god to confide in. A sage and loyal friend when sober, Hermes in his cups would say anything, then blame it on his "neutrality." He was as consistent as the summer clouds, quick to anger and quick to placidity. Eros couldn't have Hermes revealing to anyone his actual strengths. To do so would mean people expecting too much from him and he was not fully sure what his capabilities were. He wasn't gifted the All-Seeing Eye, something offered only to the gods with the greatest responsibilities, the Twelve Olympians. Yet, sometimes he sensed things, felt things before they happened. It was as if he had a myopic version of the gift and it frightened him. Still, he genuinely liked Hermes and he wished he could have someone who could advise him.

Right then, this matter with this girl was truly frustrating him. He didn't like it when his mother had tasks for him to do. He rarely questioned them, for her agitation and condescension was not worth the trouble. Eros wanted as little conflict as possible. Especially recently, when the old carnage of his youthful days was not as enjoyable as they had once been. The situation with Greece and Troy and the silliness of the beauty competition had deeply shaken the young god. For the first time he noticed the mother he respected and loved, was often shrill and unreasonable. It most likely wasn't too different from who she usually was, but this time, it perturbed him. For the reason behind the bloodshed was not the usual need for wealth and power. This was a snub so deep that the King of Sparta was going to make it his business to destroy an otherwise peaceful neighbor, all for the love of a woman.

Love.

Its ability for destruction had shaken Eros. He had seen its power on individuals, but on powerful kingdoms, it was quite another matter. Eros looked at his arrows differently. They were no longer fun toys used to torment his enemies. They were weapons that could change the destinies of both man and god for all time. Not only could it split the world, it could split Olympus, too. He decided to test his arrows on the impenetrable and passionless Hades, half convinced it would not work. If it did work, he made sure that the chosen goddess would be an appropriate mate for Hades. Matchmaking was something at which Eros was surprisingly very good. He rarely used this gift, however, except to match enemies

24

with the most improper mate. To use it for the power of good was quite a new experience for him.

After striking the god of death with an arrow as he gazed at Persephone, Eros waited for results. The days passed and there was no sign of Hades. Eros decided the arrow had failed and felt relief. Love did have its limitations after all, so he need not worry. Then rumors began to spread that the god of death had lost his senses, was neglecting his work, pacing, unable to concentrate. Diseases ran rampant, accidents went unchecked, men who should have been taken to the Underworld weren't, and those who should have remained were taken. Finally, Hades reappeared and without warning, abducted Persephone. Eros didn't know what to do. He considered rescuing her himself, but then she reappeared. Not only that, rumors spread that she had fallen in love with her macabre abductor. Eros wasn't too surprised. He had matched them for a reason. There was a goodness and sweet loneliness in the cold, impenetrable Hades. Some women, especially one with Persephone's intelligence and warmth, who always enjoyed challenge, found Hades irresistible.

However, having established the true power of his arrows, Eros now didn't know what to do. Perhaps the power was too big for him and that he should give them up for a wiser, more able god.

Instead of dealing with these questions, however, Eros decided to ignore it for the moment, and concentrate on the little tasks his mother needed him to do. The less he knew about these tasks, he soon found out, the better. Usually the punishment did not fit the crime, ranging from men who had snubbed her, to women who cursed her name, but this didn't stop him from having to fulfill them. Even Hermes knew he had to do things he didn't like sometimes.

Now, he had to fulfill another distasteful task. He promised himself not to learn more about this girl than he had to. He did not want to feel too sorry for her when he finally did meet her. Hers was a fate he would not wish on his worst enemies.

# Chapter 3

Beneath the fading starlight in the outskirts of Bromeia, morning birds were starting to sing merrily in the forest where a small pond lay quietly, its tall reeds standing like sentries guarding secrets in the water. Nothing disturbed the peace until a dark, obscure shape lifted briefly from the watery oasis. Water lilies scattered, catching on the wet tresses of a young female who did not bother to push them away. Instead, she dipped back in and disappeared again into the dark depths.

Psyche reappeared further towards the center of the pond and took a slow, deep breath. She let the droplets slide down her hair, over her dark lashes, across her cheeks, trying to absorb the soothing calmness of her surroundings. She willed her heart to slow its anxious beating, but her eyes remained troubled.

She was starting to wonder if she was human anymore. All she knew was that all her life, she had been the ugliest daughter.

Psyche of Halsted Farm on Seventh Hill had two older sisters whose beauty was renowned in Bromeia, with skin the color of polished marble, curvaceous, feminine with sunny dispositions. A common saying in town was that "Aphrodite only kissed two of Halsted's daughters." Apparently, the goddess of beauty had to run an important errand and had no time to kiss Psyche. The youngest girl was brown and skinny with awkward limbs and unmanageable, overzealous hair. Furthermore, she ran about like a barbarian in boy's clothes and never could seem to keep clean. Psyche made up for it, however, by helping to teach some of the smaller children how to read and would volunteer to read or write letters for some of the villagers. For this, she was tolerated, although not very understood.

The youngest Halsted daughter did not know why she was so different from the rest of the family. Perhaps it began when she was very young and sensed how much her father wanted a son. He always went hunting alone and would sit for hours by himself reading papyri in the dying candlelight. She suddenly wanted to fill the void for him as much as she could. As a result, while the sisters vied for their mother's affection, Psyche would follow her father, unabashedly sharing his world of literature, philosophy, history, and debate. With him, she became practiced in sports and hunting. Her mother and sister often joked that there must be a boy under her dress.

Elisa the eldest, got married to a wealthy farmer who lived in a large metropolis. Last year, the fresh and pampered eldest Halsted daughter came to visit her family and triumphantly show off her new baby girl. Psyche had just finished chasing some pigs back into their pens and when Elisa saw her youngest sister, she did not try to hide her disgust. At once, she declared that Psyche was not fit to look at and that no man would ever marry her if she went on the way she did. Psyche tried to explain that she wasn't usually this filthy, but Elisa brushed her away like a buzzing gnat. Then, as if the idea just occurred to her, she generously offered to take Psyche to Pella for a year and teach her refinement.

The prospect filled Psyche with horror. Although the people of Bromeia were not always kind, they were used to Psyche's ways and tolerated her. She could handle the harmless ridicule of her family and villagers, but she shuddered at what a city as sophisticated and elegant as Pella would think of her.

Her mother, however, thought it was a wonderful idea. Psyche was sixteen and women her age, her mother declared, were often on their second or third child.

"Don't you want to get married, Psyche?" Elisa questioned sharply. "And not have to burden your parents for your keep? They are old, you know. If you truly loved them, you would make more of an effort to find a man who can take care of you."

"Of course, I love my family! And I try to do as much as I can to help around here."

"Utter nonsense!" Her mother protested.

"I hunted and killed the very boar you are filling your belly with right now."

"What's a little bit of meat? I gave you life! And all you do is take from your poor father and me! All the scolding and teaching I give you and no results. It's your father's fault, letting her run wild. I've seen wild pigs cleaner than that one."

27

Psyche turned to her father for some help but realized that he was reading a parchment and was not even paying attention to the conversation.

The argument had been one her mother had made countless times, but this time Eliza and her mother had struck a nerve. Just that afternoon while out in the woods hunting with her father, he suddenly complained of pain in his side and had to rest. His pallor frightened Psyche. For the first time, she noticed how much older he looked. He felt better after a few minutes of rest but they headed home immediately. The incident was still haunting her.

Then, there was little Flavia cooing in Elisa's arms.

Seeing how taken Psyche was by Flavia, Elisa hit her other weak point with the precision of a master archer. "Don't you want to experience being a mother?"

The effect was surprising, even for Psyche. How nice it would be to have a child to love, to teach about the world and read poetry with. Yet, she never believed that anyone would ever want to marry her. Not only was she not pretty, her family had very little to offer. Elisa's marriage was the stuff of fantasy. Granted her husband was twice as old as she, and short and bald to boot, but she was well taken care of and now had this beautiful little soul to call her own.

It only took a few more days to break Psyche's resolve. After much thought, the youngest Halsted daughter agreed to go, convinced that smoothing out some of her rough edges could help her find a kind man who would find her little quirks pleasing.

But the year was long and Psyche's transformation had been a painful one. Her sister tried to scrape the brown off of her naturally olive skin and found it hopeless. Some nights, Psyche would be unable to sleep due to the burning sensation on her face, neck, and arms. The next morning, the dark shadows that formed under her eyes caused Elisa to have a fit.

Then, there was her hair. Elisa and servants tried to untangle her mess of curls and, in a rage, ended up cutting much of it. For a while, Psyche truly did look like a boy, with frizzy strands sticking straight up. But at least the brush was able to go through.

"A daily brush," Elisa ordered firmly. "You must never forget this or it will become an impossible bird's nest again. I don't care how exhausted you are. Every day!"

Then, there were Elisa's homemade creams that she used in the hope of lightening Psyche's skin. Instead, it made her face break out in horrible, angry red bumps.

Looking into the mirror, Psyche could not see any improvement. Her hair looked like a boy's, her skin was red and blotchy, her eyes were constantly drooping and tired. But she did like the smell of the soaps her sister used, and her dark hair was starting to grow back with red and blond streaks mixed in with the brown. It was strange, but she did not question it.

Teaching Psyche mannerisms, however, was an even tougher task for Elisa. She first took her little sister to town so that she could be introduced to the more elegant ladies and observe the grace and etiquette necessary for an entitled woman. These meetings were so dull and Psyche was so sleep deprived that she would often nod off. She would then wake up to her hissing older sister who would order her to run an errand so she could stop embarrassing her.

Elisa did not realize that running errands was Psyche's favorite thing to do. Only then was she free to explore the bustling city on her own, listening to the discussions in the Acropolis, observing the exciting curiosity of people from places she had only read, and goods being sold that she had never seen. One vendor sold healing remedies from all over the world. They included vials of Cyclops' tears, and powder made of dragon claws. Everything had a story, which the vendor was always happy to tell to his wide-eyed audience. Psyche noticed that the stories seemed to change every day and realized that they must be made up. Still, she loved listening to the vendor talk because the stories were so vivid and entertaining.

Then, there was a merchant who sold unique contraptions, the designs given to him, he said, by Hermes himself who visited his dreams. Psyche would spend hours trying to understand how some of them worked. At one point, a little peasant boy had accidentally broken a wooden nutcracker. Seeing the panic in his eyes, Psyche went over and tried to help him. She used an unbroken machine as a model and figured out how to reattach the broken pieces. The little boy was grateful and together, they left the vendor without anyone being the wiser.

The best thing about Pella, however, was the forum where Psyche could listen to town debates and get updates on the battles that went on in distant lands. She loved the vivid stories of heroic deeds, with brave men who had fallen and the stir of controversy that seemed to accompany every speech. The war in Troy was especially heart breaking, for many had strong opinions and fights would often break out.

Psyche was grateful for her cropped hair, for the forum was not open to women, so she had to go disguised as a man with a long heavy gray cloak covering her from head to foot. She loved the freedom the disguise allotted her. She met poets and musicians who told stories in verse that mesmerized as well as brought Psyche to tears. When her hair began growing back, she found a way to tuck it in to continue the ruse.

Then, there was the local library where hours would melt away. When the rain prevented further exploration, the rows and rows of papyri available for her perusal was all she needed to keep her riveted.

Her sister made sure these activities were punished by a long lecture about the uselessness of a clever mind, and then a chore meant to humble and humiliate her. Psyche had come to realize that Elisa brought her to Pella specifically to use her as an extra servant. She was the perfect nursemaid for Flavia. Elisa did not trust Flavia's nurses and often sent them scurrying away in fright. But Psyche loved playtime with Flavia who always had dried leaves caught in her blond curls and never seemed to judge. Flavia didn't call her ugly or hopeless. Flavia just cooed and laughed at her funny faces.

One thing that her sister was able to interest Psyche in were clothes. It was a surprising interest, for she was sure it would bore her as much as everything else, but the colors and textures found in the city were like nothing she had seen or felt before, and they were finally clothes that fit her properly.

When Psyche was allowed to choose the color, she opted for natural soft pastels that made her skin tone look like bronze shimmering in the sun.

Hers was not a standard beauty, however, and it was missed on her sister who simply shook her head and sighed. Her skin was still blotchy from another one of her failed creams.

"I have done my best. You are improved, but you are quite hopeless. You will never eat enough to get my figure and no amount of scrubbing can get your skin as creamy and white as mine. But at least you are presentable. And I never noticed your green eyes. They're almost pretty, if a little too big. What do you think, husband?"

The truth was, her husband was quite stunned by Psyche. Even with the right side of her face looking painfully inflamed, he was kicking himself for not having seen the diamond in the rough and choosing her for his wife instead. But he also was not foolish enough to tell his wife this who had been favoring him quite well these past few months.

"She is… much improved. You must not compare a dove to a sparrow, my dear."

Elisa laughed and squeezed his hand. "Very well, Psyche, you may go home now. No doubt, Mama and Papa have missed you sorely, Papa especially."

Psyche was already out the door to get her things before her sister could even finish speaking. She barely heard Elisa call out to her, "What did I say about wide strides? And are you skipping steps again? Really, I do not know why I even bother with that ungrateful hoyden."

Saying good-bye to Flavia had been more difficult. Psyche kissed the tiny toddler farewell sending a prayer for her health and happiness and hugging her a little too tightly. She tried not to feel hurt when the little girl pulled away. At the sight of a fluffy kitten under a pile of straw, Flavia quickly forgot her aunt and scurried away.

The journey home took several days and Psyche had to travel it alone as Elisa was not feeling well. During that time, Psyche felt the stinging on her face lessen as she refused to continue the cream regimen that Elisa had insisted upon for an entire year. She had not had a chance to look at herself before arriving at the house, but when her mother saw her, she began to wonder if it was truly that bad.

31

Psyche touched her hair self-consciously as Hermena continued to stare.

Her father, however, greeted her with great warmth, not seeming to notice any change at all, and insisted she come to the library and see his new collection of insects. Psyche breathed a sigh of relief.

That night, they had a visitor, an old friend she had known for years. Claudius arrived, loud and gregarious as usual, but when he saw Psyche, he tripped on their rug and apologized nervously. For a while, he wouldn't do anything except stare at her. It was as if he were in a trance. When she asked him if he were ill, he gave a quivering laugh and said that if he was it was the most pleasant fever he'd ever felt!

That night, she stared at her reflection as if for the first time.

The red bumps from the lightening creams were gone leaving a smooth familiar face. Yet, it was also different, older than before, stronger somehow and her eyes looked bigger, almost luminous. Still, it was just a face. Two eyes, a nose and a mouth like everyone else's. Psyche shook her head and went to bed deciding that Claudius must have indulged in too much wine again.

A few days later, her father organized a gathering where there was to be a serious discussion about a new poet and his impact on the kingdom. Psyche had already read his work, formed her own opinion, and was excited to share her perspective as well as listen to the others. However, after she finished helping her mother in the kitchen and arrived to join the debates, no one wanted to talk about the poet anymore. The atrium fell silent and the men's mouths dropped open.

Psyche waited, not knowing what to do. Claudius was the first to approach her and take her hand. But he addressed the room, not her. For a moment, she felt as if she wasn't really there and that everything was happening to someone else.

"What did I tell you, men? Does she not shame the statues of Aphrodite?"

Suddenly they were all flocking to her, asking her about her trip to Pella, declaring she was the most beautiful thing they had ever seen, wanting to tell her how much land they owned and how many important people they knew, and when she pleaded that she was tired and would like to sit, two men began to fight over who would sit next to her. Her mother rushed in and simply stared at the debacle for several seconds before banging two pots together and ordering all the men home.

When they had all left, a strange look crossed Hermena's face.

"What's swimming in that head of yours, my dear?" Her husband had not missed it.

"Why nothing at all, my love."

The next day in town, however, when shopping for a new goat, Hermena heard the comments made by the locals. Her daughter had created quite a sensation. Everyone was talking about her ethereal, newfound beauty that had the men fighting like Trojans and Greeks. Making up her mind, Psyche's mother came home with silks and jewels for Psyche's new wardrobe.

"What happened to the goat?" Her husband asked her when she returned with an armful of feminine things.

"Goats do not give as much return on investment as a beautiful child. The gods are finally smiling on us!"

Although their fortune was much improved from Elisa's marriage, there was no end to Psyche's potential. Instead of doing their usual chores, the women worked painstakingly on sewing new garments for Psyche. They worked for hours and Claudia plead a headache halfway through.

"Will none of these dresses be for me?" She mourned.

"What need have you for anymore dresses?" Hermena retorted. "You've trunks full of them that you never wear and what good has it done you? Not even a single suitor vying for your hand. Meanwhile, our poor Psyche has been suffering without all these years."

"Claudia, you can have this one I'm making. I haven't finished the hem yet, but when it's done—" Psyche offered.

"Nonsense," Hermena snapped. "Do you know how much that material cost? You will all stop your chatter and finish before sun rise as planned." Meanwhile, Claudia's bitterness increased with each passing hour until Psyche could almost feel her glare digging into her with every stab of the needle. Miserable, Psyche refused to look up the rest of the night.

That morning, while the rest of the family were still asleep, Psyche walked to her favorite pond deep in the heart of the woods where there was no path. She had come ever since she discovered it as a little girl of eleven years. Here, she could swim and pretend that she was a water nymph, beautiful and gay, with carefree immortality stretching endlessly before her. There was no one to make fun of her or to point out her failings. There was no one to glare hatefully at her. Here, the reeds played music to her and the sun kissed her face in unprejudiced adoration. The cool, refreshing water made her fingers and toes tingle and washed away the anger, shock, and weariness of the last several days.

Beauty.

It was such an odd thing. All her life, she had insisted she never wanted it, did not need it, but deep inside, she wished she were beautiful. Who didn't? Good things always happened to beautiful people. Strong, handsome, and noble men fell in love with lovely maidens. Beautiful women at the market always got a little extra grain when they smiled sweetly and were given discounts without ever needing to haggle. They were always so certain of themselves, so sure of their place in the world.

Now, having been gifted this rare and precious commodity, Psyche was beginning to wonder whether it was more of a curse than a blessing. The hostile glares from other women were extremely alarming. She could not speak to a man without a woman suddenly appearing to put a possessive hand on his sleeve. She could not smile at a man without him immediately asking if he could speak to her father. "About what?" she had asked the first time it happened with a tailor. "About our engagement, of course," he replied. Dumbfounded, she shook her head and stumbled away.

Psyche had never felt so watched, so exposed as men and women followed her every move, for completely different reasons. She found herself making extra sure that her dress was arranged properly, that her hair was not too badly askew. The women were sure to point out and snicker at every flaw. Once, she had a bit of straw on her hair and no one would tell her. Instead, the ladies jeered amongst themselves until a fellow gallantly pulled the dry plant off her head. When she thanked him, he asked if he could speak to her father and followed her for miles even as she told him again and again that she was not interested.

Then there was the flattery that never felt sincere. Sometimes she felt the men would use her just to start a jealous spar with another man who had slighted him about something else. Nothing was what it seemed and Psyche seemed to be the cause of every ounce of mischief in the village.

It was impossible to tell who truly valued her and who was simply pretending. She was frustrated. Even Lucius the Pious, her old friend and a well-respected horse trader and renowned philosopher, Psyche's favorite of all of her father's companions despite their very different viewpoints, and the youngest at twenty-two winters, was no longer recognizable. His personality had changed. It was as if he lost the very brain she had admired most about him. Psyche was most displeased that he did not remember arguing with her about the persecution of Prometheus no more than a year ago.

Prometheus was an immortal who stole fire from the gods to give to humanity. As punishment, he was chained to a wall and fed upon by vultures. Being immortal, his suffering was eternal. Lucius tried to change the subject, not willing to hear anything he deemed blasphemous, which to him could be as simple as muttering "Great Zeus!" in vain. But last night, he did concede, more than he ever did before, that all were entitled to their own opinion.

He then raved about her good nature and that it was only a reflection of her truly kind heart that she would wish to forgive the ills of men like Prometheus. Few things fired up Psyche's temper, but injustice was top on her list.

"Ills? Ills?" Psyche grew hotter by the minute. "He stole fire from the gods and gave it to man so that we could be warm and our babies not freeze to death. He sacrificed himself for us and is now chained to a rock, being eaten by buzzards for all of eternity. What illness could he have except the illness of too much love for ungrateful men such as you?"

"My dear, Psyche," Lucius eyes hardened somewhat at the insult, "You're causing a spectacle."

"I only have to breathe to cause a spectacle in this crowd!" Psyche stopped herself before she said something regretful. "I'm sorry. I have a headache. I would like everyone to clear the room please."

When several came to offer assistance, she raised her voice even more and insisted they go at once. Lucius lingered, believing that she had purposely emptied the room so that they could be alone together. She had to tell him in the coldest of manners that this was not the case. The crushed look that crossed his eyes would have tormented the old Psyche and pressed upon her conscience, but she reminded herself that he was stubborn and unjust. He will warm himself with a fire tonight and not think twice about the poor, legendary immortal, Prometheus, who gave up everything to provide that fire for him.

In Lucius's eyes, the gods were always right.

Psyche did not think so. Perhaps her arrogance will send her straight to Tartarus, but if the gods were so admirable, then how could they let so many good people suffer? Laws should not be so rigid that they don't take to account the complexity of a situation.

As Psyche pulled herself up from the pond, she was excited to see the sun was finally peeking out of some low clouds and was starting to kiss her face. She loved drying her skin in the sun. She suspected that was why her skin kept turning such a bronze shade that had been so displeasing to her sister, but alas, she would never give up this one pleasure simply standing completely still and naked while the sun dried the cold droplets from her still tingling skin. As she stood drying, she tried to picture her husband in this imaginary small cabin, but saw only a shadowy figure, faceless but warm, always warm like a hearth.

Just before the rays of Helios could peak above the clouds and beam excitedly against the bright blue sky, a sudden thundercloud appeared from nowhere and veiled the disappointed sun. It began raining instantaneously and Psyche quickly donned on her tunic knowing that from a distance, most would think she was just another hunter and let her be. She was disappointed that the morning wasn't going as she would have liked, but when the huge drops of rain splattered against her already wet head, she laughed at its audacity. The rain was a good substitute for the sun. Soon, her body was as thoroughly wet as it had been when she first got out of the water. She didn't mind this at all.

# Chapter 4

Eros was up before dawn and pacing quietly on a rooftop, waiting for the town to wake up. Slowly, the narrow alleyways began to fill with traders and shopkeepers, and the smell of fresh flat bread and roasting meats filled the air. It was early, but he needed to find this mysterious girl quickly and he had no leads. Dark clouds threatened the weathered roofs. In a few hours, he expected a downpour. Eros did not intend to fly back to Olympus with wet wings. He shuddered at the prospect.

Scrambling over the rooftops, he searched for a good spot to eavesdrop on conversations. He needed to get a name at least. Aphrodite did not think to provide such "unimportant" details. What *was* important was how this horrid human proclaimed herself to be more beautiful than the owner of the Golden Apples, and how disgusting such arrogance was. Eros sighed, remembering his mother's shrieks. "Find the most haughty chit in Bromeia and ruin her. Ruin her!" This was his mother's orders, shouted at the top of her lungs just last night before she stalked away, almost kicking the white minx on the marble ground that almost tripped her. Fortunately, the rodent escaped her wrath.

A hot sizzling sound caught Eros's attention. Instantly, his mouth watered as he spied a meat pie from a nearby vender. He changed himself back to his shepherd's disguise then scrambled off the roof and walked casually towards the friendly baker.

Pie in hand, he inhaled the spices appreciatively and dug in. As he devoured the flavorful crust, he continued to listen to conversations, trying to blend into his surroundings. By the time he had licked the last of the gravy, there was still no word about the girl. He did learn that the blacksmith's daughter had run away with a foot soldier and the family declared her dead to them. Also, the local tailor was caught cheating at dice again and there was talk that he would get his finger removed. The baker's wife declared loudly for all to hear that the punishment was well deserved.

Eros sighed in exasperation. Now that his belly was full, he needed to focus. But for a young lady rumored to be more beautiful than any goddess, she was not as well talked about as he would have expected.

Finally, he spied two young men chatting while their horses slurped noisily from a public fountain. One suddenly mentioned how pompous the girl who lived on Seventh Hill was, now that she had returned from the big city. The one who spoke was fair haired and slim while his companion was dark and burly.

"Do you mean Claudia?"

"No, her sister, Psyche. Claudia never left Bromeia."

"I know that, but I didn't think you could be talking about Psyche. She is not pompous one bit, Lucius! You're just upset because she won that debate about that fire-stealing fellow. She's a sharp one, that girl."

The blond man frowned and washed his hands as if the water irritated him. "I don't know if that is such an admirable trait in a woman. And, I wouldn't say that she won. Shooed me away before I could make my point, more like it."

"She certainly did win! She changed my mind right the minute she defended that little thieving immortal. The fellow did do us a service disobeying the gods to help mankind. You're just too pious to see it. As for Psyche being a bit edgy last night, well who wouldn't be with so many less worthy men buzzing all around her. Why, she is worth ten of us mere mortals. She should have been a goddess!"

Eros stooped down as if to wash his hands as well. At last, a name! And by the sound of it, she could certainly be a problem for Olympus.

Lucius was now glaring at the larger, more burlesque man. He did not approve besmirching gods. Eros appreciated that.

"You should mind your tongue, Claudius."

Claudius looked around with a worried expression. "Why, do you see one of the gods among us now?"

Eros froze, feeling the man's eyes on him briefly, but then he heard a cackle of laughter. Lucius moved away, insulted, and began preparing his horse for departure. "You're not supposed to be able to see them. If you see them, the force of their beauty could instantly blind you, or drive you to insanity."

"How convenient," was Claudius's deriding response. "They're there, but you can't see them. And we're supposed to honor them, even though they kick us in the arse day in and day out. Just the other day I prayed for sun so that I could go hunting with my boys and what does good old Apollo give me? Rain and more rain. I say, to Tartarus with the gods! If I think a prettier one walks among us, then good for mankind! We're better off without the lot of them."

Lucius gasped and immediately said a prayer to the heavens. "Claudius! Such talk will bring a curse upon the whole village!"

"Curses, indeed. So what if I prefer gazing at Psyche to the statues of Aphrodite? A real flesh and blood woman, now that's a treat! Not one made of stone or marble, and not one made up by superstitious fools like you. And from what I hear, I am not the only one."

They were starting to collect quite a crowd and a few men were starting to join in.

"If you're talking about Psyche of Seventh Hill, I am in full agreement with Claudius."

"Aye!" shouted another voice. "I saw her the other day. I've never seen anything that more resembled a goddess in my life."

"You are truly mad!" Lucius cried out. "No mortal woman can be considered divine. What you are saying is sacrilege!"

"Call it what you like," Claudius shrugged. "But, maybe it's nice to think of mankind as more than just a plaything for the gods. Maybe we can be as mighty as they. Ever think of that? Psyche makes me think like that. When I look at her, she makes me think I could be more than who I am. Because she's a mortal, just like me. And she makes me proud to be a mortal!"

"Ludicrous. We are nothing compared to the gods and if you don't watch out, evil will fall upon you and our entire village!"

"Oh, you and your superstitions, Lucius," scoffed someone in the crowd.

Claudius, excited about the men who were all in agreement, laughed derisively. "And why should we listen to you? You are not a priest, Lucius. You're a horse trader. Though obviously you would rather have your head in the arse of Zeus than between the breasts of a beautiful woman."

Lucius threw the first punch and Eros moved away just as the crowds around him erupted with excitement. Eros turned and looked towards a cluster of hills where this Psyche's house supposedly lay. He knew she had to be the woman he sought. She certainly was a potential source of trouble. He needed to get rid of her quickly.

He found a secluded alleyway where he could change himself. If he weren't in such a rush, he wouldn't dare attempt to do this with so many people around, but the crowd was so excited by the brawl in the middle of the square, they didn't even notice the very brief flash of light as Eros shot up into the air.

When Eros reached the seventh of a row of green sloping hills, he saw a simple farmhouse that was much smaller than he expected. He found it hard to believe that anything of such resplendent beauty could dwell in it. Hiding in the trees, he spied an older woman carrying water from a well. She could have been pretty at one time but her face now looked withered from long hours in the sun and her green eyes were sharp, like shards of broken glass.

Eros saw a younger figure approach the woman. He moved closer only to see that the golden haired girl was much too plain to be the rumored Psyche. This must be Claudia, her sister.

Finally, the older woman spoke aloud the question Eros wanted most answered, "Where is Psyche?"

Claudia shrugged, and the moody pout on her face revealed more than she could know. "Who knows? Probably still sleeping."

"Ah well, such beauty needs as much sleep as she can get."

"Well, maybe if I could sleep a bit longer instead of working like a slave, I could be beautiful too!"

"Dear child, of course you are beautiful. I honestly don't know what the men could see in such a skinny, dark thing, but such are the opinions of men, unpredictable. Her looks just happen to be the fashion these days. A preferred flavor of the month. But you, my dearest, dearest girl, you are a classic."

"Then why does no man look at me when she's near. I mean, even Lucius…"

"Lucius, pah! What is a poor horse trader to Psyche's beauty? No, no, Lucius will never be good enough for her. He should settle fine with you."

41

Eros, shaking his head at the conversation, flew quickly to the window of a bedroom and saw that there was no one there. There was no one in any of the bedrooms. Further survey convinced him that Psyche was not in the house.

Where had she gone? Could she have run off with someone? A man? Did she already have a lover? She was, after all, a mere mortal woman with needs. If she destroyed her own reputation, then perhaps Eros did not need to intervene and the world would soon discard her. Eros never quite understood the odd double standards humans put upon their women, but it was of no concern to him if she saved him some trouble.

He could have waited for her to return, but that was not Eros's way. He was an expert tracker. He saw how she had climbed out of her bedroom window, and where her soft sandals disturbed the field grass. Following her trail, he found himself deep in the woods. He became more certain that he would find the errant girl in the embrace of some poor blacksmith's son or other. His mother had so much more faith in these humans than they truly deserved. Surely they would cause their own demise without any assistance from the gods.

Aware of his mission, Eros spied a giant, hideous male boar digging for truffles not too far from him. Knowing that animals sensed gods far better than humans did, Eros was swift with his arrow and struck the boar. The hideous gray animal immediately smelled him and came scampering, enthralled with his new mate. Having accomplished this small part of the tasteless mission, Eros went on his way with the hog faithfully trailing after him.

As Eros stooped to more closely observe Psyche's tracks, the hog snorted and tried to smell his feet. Eros sighed and pet the unsightly swine.

"Never fear, you will be absolutely adored very soon, my unworthy friend. When little Psyche falls in love with you, she will be deemed positively unhinged and no man will want her."

Eros sighed at the unpleasant business. It was one of Aphrodite's favorite methods for revenge and one of the more disturbing.

The deeper Eros went into the woods, the more certain he was that two lovers would never go to such lengths to meet, even in secret. There were many romantic groves that were completely ignored, including a spot under the shade of the most delightful mulberries not too far from the edge of the woods. However, the trail was taking him to a much more secluded area and when it stopped, he was certain that he had made a mistake since it ended at a little pool. Had she fallen in? Did she climb up? Was she truly a goddess and flew?

Eros was relieved when he spied a water nymph floating just ahead of him. He was going to ask her if she had seen a woman come by when he suddenly paused and looked more closely. She was not, in actuality, a water nymph.

No, the lilies in her hair were accidental. The sodden, multi-colored tresses were rare in a mortal and blended well with the reeds and grass with streaks of pale yellow, dusty brown, auburn and red.

Psyche at last!

Eros crouched behind some shrubbery and pulled out an arrow, ready to fulfill his task as quickly as possible so that he could get to more important matters. This was all terribly distasteful as it was. Eros had been mildly impressed with the hair, for he had never seen its like on a human woman, but he couldn't see anything else. She would not be an easy shot in the water, and missing and startling her may destroy his chances, so he had to wait for her to finish.

Eros looked impatiently at the sun. He truly did not have all day.

He moved quietly to a more advantageous position and waited. He felt something rub against his leg and impatiently pushed the squealing boar away from him. The time was not right for the boar to cross the young woman's path just yet.

Finally the girl was lifting herself from the water. The tint of her skin gave Eros a pause. It was something unexpected in these regions, something he saw more in the southern parts, but its consistency and tone was quite intriguing, not quite gold, and not quite bronze. Different, altogether. Her shoulders were straight and powerful. In fact, they mirrored Athena more than Aphrodite in their strength and athleticism. Her hair covered most of her back, with only a hint of a shapely derriere that Eros could not stop himself from lingering upon. He allowed his eyes to fall to her legs, long, powerful, and curving to calves so balanced and perfect, he could almost believe he was staring at a statue, not a woman. Even at this distance, he could see that she was wonderfully proportioned. Eros found that the hand at the bow went suddenly quite still.

He wanted to see her face. Besides, the potency of the arrow would be strongest if it hits her heart.

At last, she turned to face the sun, wringing out the pond from her hair. Her eyes were downcast and she seemed thoroughly absorbed in the task at hand.

Eros was a little shaken by the clear picture of her perfect breasts, firm and round cresting in sublime balance before her. Her face was of an exquisite shape, broader than most faces with full, even lips, a narrow but strong nose and eyes that were closed in the enjoyment of pushing her hair back and feeling the breeze.

Eros steadied his heart, shook his head, and told himself she was prettier, nay, more beautiful than most, but she was just another mortal, one that apparently was becoming too big in the head and causing mischief in the village, turning pious men sacrilegious, starting brawls for no good reason. She needed to learn her place. There was no time for ogling pretty girls.

Eros tightened his grip on his arrow, annoyed that his hand was not as steady as it had been earlier. But it was a mere hiccup. The wind was just so and if he—.

Just then, the sun was starting to peek through a cloud and Psyche's eyes opened slowly, a soft, gentle smile creeping up her face. Eros saw a color of such dazzling green reminding him of Elysian pastures, lush mossy forest beds, its radiance pulling at something so buried and frozen within him that its stirring felt like a physical pain. He imagined himself looking directly at such eyes and drowning in their warmth and understanding. In their intelligence, wisdom, and depth of feeling.

The jealous boar cried out and ran between Eros's legs. The arrow fell instantly from his hand and in trying to catch it, grazed his palm. Eros gasped and looked down at the gash in his hand knowing that he was in great danger if he looked up and gazed at Psyche one more time. He cursed the wretched boar that had scampered away, careful to keep his eyes down and closed. He needed to wait until she left. He knew better than anyone how his arrows worked. If he could keep his eyes closed and escape without laying eyes on anyone, the poison will leave his system and he would not be lost.

But he heard her moving. He knew she was there, smiling, happy and radiant. Were those eyes real?

Without another thought, Eros braced himself. Making a decision he knew would alter his entire life, Eros opened his eyes and looked squarely upon the woman he had been sent to destroy.

# Chapter 5

At that exact moment, the sun was spreading throughout her face, throughout her body and Psyche truly did resemble a shimmering goddess, her head lifted to the sky, her hands falling at her side in perfect naked shamelessness, confidence, and beauty.

Eros thought he had died. The full impact of his desire almost caused him to rush forward and sweep Psyche away the way Hades had swept away his Persephone. For the first time, Eros understood the potency of his arrows.

Suddenly, there was a noise to his left and a group of woodsmen were heading towards the clearing. Psyche was too enthralled with the sun to hear them. Eros looked more closely at Apollo's chariot that was starting to crest above the clouds and catch sight of the lovely maiden who was offering him a full view of her body. Enraged with jealousy for the sun god, Eros bid the wind god, Zephyr, who owed him a favor, to push a storm cloud this way and blind Apollo momentarily just before he could see the golden tips of Psyche's gorgeous breasts. Eros's mouth went dry as rain immediately started falling on her skin. She reacted swiftly, swooping on her clothes and rushing away from the pond in his direction. For a moment, Eros's breath caught as she neared him. But she did not see him, did not even sense him, and flew past him leaving only the smell of her delicious hair at her wake.

Eros knew he shouldn't follow her. He knew that the only way to reduce the potency of his arrows was to avoid any sort of contact or interaction with the object of desire for as long as possible. Even if it took years or centuries. He was an immortal, he had the time. The craving would eventually go away. This was the only antidote to his arrows. Distance, time, and perhaps another woman. Lots and lots of other women. But the antidote was apparently the hardest of all to swallow.

Eros found himself doggedly following this beautiful mortal and when it looked like she was going to cross paths with the dangerous woodsmen, he made a quick decision and changed himself immediately to his shepherd disguise.

Psyche was enjoying the sound of the rain and the excited frenzy of her own racing feet. Goodness, it felt good to run again! *No wide strides*, she remembered her sister bellowing at her. Indeed, how is one supposed to get anywhere without wide strides? She jumped over a puddle, laughing at the splash she made.

She did not see the woodsmen until they were only a few feet from her.

"Well, well, well. What have we here? A young runt got away from his hunting party, did he?"

"Where you heading to in such a rush, lad? You almost rolled over us."

Psyche clutched her sodden shirt, the cold causing her breasts to peak like berries against the soft cotton. She quickly tried to cover up with her cloak but the astute eye of the closest woodsman had not missed it. She pulled her hood closer so that it hid most of her face and she deepened her voice trying to disguise it.

"I am simply heading home. There is a cave about half a mile north of here. You should find good shelter there."

"We are much obliged. But, we are not quite familiar with these woods. Perhaps you would be so good as to lead us directly there."

Psyche knew this would be a mistake and the woodsmen's leering eyes had not been lost upon her. As she hesitated, one of the men reached over and pulled her hood down and all gasped with pleasure at the sight of her tumbling hair and face.

Psyche glared at the men. "Let me pass." It was a cold command that usually worked for her. Today was not one of her luckier days. The woodsmen's eyes narrowed at her haughty tone.

"Oh, lookie here, boys. Suddenly we are to obey her like she is some great goddess."

"Hardly that," scoffed another. "No respectable woman would be out and about walking alone dressed like that."

"Which is why she is not alone."

When the voice spoke behind her, Psyche jumped at the sound. She felt like she could handle the woodsmen, for she was a swift runner and she was not unarmed. But a fourth man who could sneak up behind her was another matter. It took her only a few moments to realize that he was a shepherd and not a woodsman and that he did not know these men.

"Does this one belong to you?"

"Indeed," the young man answered to her surprise. "She is my sister and was helping me gather some sheep that had escaped this morning. You men would be so kind as to allow us to pass."

He moved in front of her, not glancing at her direction but subtly creating a barrier between her and the men.

There was an authority in his voice, but it was not as icy and demanding as hers had been. Where she had to compensate true authority for the sound of it, this man needed only a level voice that was used to being obeyed.

Psyche still expected some resistance, for the young man, though strong in voice and certainly well filled out in his herder's frock, was still very young and did not look well matched for three brawny woodsmen. She was standing behind him, however, and she could not see the warning in his blue eyes now dark with a hidden aggression. She did not see the authoritarian air that spoke of something larger than what appeared. The lead woodsmen looked back at her, the desire in his eyes warring with fear, then back at the shepherd. Psyche gripped her short sword tightly, prepared to fight if she had to, but was surprised when the middle woodsmen shrugged.

"Keep a tight rein on that one. She needs to watch that haughty mouth of hers."

"Her mouth is her own," responded her rescuer softly, but the woodsmen were already on their way. Eros's thoughts, however, were occupied with the beauty of the mouth upon the face that was now only a few feet from him. He did not have to turn to remember its full softness. When he did allow himself to look at her, he was not prepared for the pleasure of her beauty. She really was unearthly. He could feel the poison of the arrow gripping his heart and strangling all reason out of it. It was hard to focus, hard to breathe.

Psyche stared up at him, her face unimpressed.

This stranger had come from nowhere. He was tall, broad shouldered as she had determined before. His features were fine, but not anything out of the ordinary. She had been surrounded by so many of her father's friends that she had forgotten what truly young men looked like. This one did not appear much older than she was. She supposed he could be handsome, but his clothes were nearly threadbare, and his sandals worn and muddy. Furthermore, the closest sheep field was miles from here and belonged to Claudius, one of her father's friends. She did not believe his story that he was looking for errant livestock, not all the way here.

Psyche did not let up on her firm grip of her short sword. His appearance had been convenient if anything. If he proved to be a thief, well, she had nothing to offer him. If he wanted something else, she would not give in without a proper fight.

"Thank you," her voice was stiff. "You did not have to lie for me."

She did not bother to hide her wariness. He had lied about being her sister and he lied about looking for livestock. He was capable of anything.

For a moment, he stared at her, as if he was surprised she could speak. Then his eyes softened and he gave a look so warm and intimate that she almost took a step back.

As if sensing her alarm, he immediately flashed her a smile that sent sharp bolts akin to lightning in an area above her stomach, at the same time, putting her at ease.

"What must you think of me?" His voice was different from the voice he used with the woodsmen. It was gentle, like a bubbling brook, soothing, warm, laughter hidden within like a treasure chest. "You do not even know who I am, yet the first words you heard me utter was a lie. Clearly, I am not to be trusted."

He placed a hand to his heart, as much to steady it as to symbolize respect. His guileless blue eyes could not be anything but pure innocence.

Psyche, despite her doubts, could not help returning the smile. Disarmed, she unconsciously loosened her grip on the sword.

"Clearly not," she responded.

"I am in a very difficult situation, then. I am certain that I am worthy of trust and friendship, but how could I ever convince you of this now?"

"Well, being that you had only told a falsehood to save me from a fate possibly worse than death, I believe some leniency is in order. But, I must warn you now, I am not always so forgiving."

The rain had miraculously stopped, and Psyche looked up at the peaking sun with gratitude.

"See, this is a good omen!" she cried out, her smile reflecting her relief as well as her joy. "The weather approves of my decision!"

She thought she saw the young man swallow perceptively but she couldn't be sure for he smiled a carefree smile again and tilted his head slightly.

"I must know your name."

*But you already know it.* She thought to herself. Psyche did not know why she was so sure of this. Perhaps it was that look he had given her earlier, the one that made her think he was an old childhood friend that she had long forgotten but he hadn't.

"I am Psyche."

"I am Erik."

Psyche did not know the name and smiled and gave a little curtsy, which was strange since she was in men's wear.

"Erik. It is a foreign name. And yet, you dress like a shepherd and shepherds are not known to be nomadic people."

The young man blinked. He seemed taken aback.

"You seem to know much about shepherds."

"I read much," she declared, watching to see if this repulsed him.

"Alas, you are at an advantage. I do not read at all."

Psyche was surprised by her disappointment. Illiteracy was no surprise in a poor, uneducated shepherd. It was not like she was hoping to marry him. How silly she suddenly felt. They had only just met! Even so, he seemed like a kind young man and very pleasant to the eyes. She found that she was not ready to part company. Besides, what if the woodsmen came back?

"I was not lying," Eros lied. "I really was looking for an errant sheep. But alas, I got bored of the job and decided to wander a bit away from home. I live in some pastures a very long way from here near the town of Pella. It was not well done of me, but my father is used to my ways. He knows I am curious by nature and will be back home when I'm ready."

"He is quite forgiving, then."

"He is the best of fathers. He understands what it's like to be a young man, restless, yearning to see the world. When the time comes, I will take over the pastures, find a wife, and settle into my life, but now is not that time."

They came upon a clearing where Erik took her to a small donkey munching on a nearby tuft of grass. It was tied to a mulberry tree whose fruit was growing white and luscious, weighing the tree down so low that the branches created a canopy. The flecks of light peeping through the leaves danced on Erik's smiling face.

"Your donkey?" she asked.

"Indeed. Her name is Juno."

"What a strange name for an ass."

"But more appropriate than you know. Perhaps you would allow me to give you a ride home."

"On your donkey?" She looked uncertain.

"She is much more stout than she looks and quite comfy. But, I understand if you are frightened."

"Frightened of a donkey? I'll have you know I've ridden much more violent creatures than that!"

Erik smiled enigmatically. "Then, it is the owner you are afraid of? I still have not won your trust."

His eyes were full of something Psyche could not quite define, but a warmth spread throughout her body. She had never experienced anything like it. A second ago, he was just a lowly shepherd, friendly and innocent. Now, she was suddenly very aware of her damp clothes and a danger from which she did not think she wanted to run.

Psyche considered what a picture the two of them would make on the tiny creature and chuckled. She had learned about risk-taking during her time in Pella, and knew that interesting and new experiences should be embraced whenever possible. For some reason, she did not want to part ways with her rescuer. His company was bemusing, different from her father's friends, different from anyone she had met. And he did rescue her after all. Besides, Psyche always trusted her instincts, and there was something very appealing and unaffected about this spirited young man with a smile that made the sun look paltry.

"If you are certain that both of our weights wouldn't kill her..."

"Never. She has the stamina of a centaur. Just look at those fierce eyes!"

The donkey continued to munch slowly on mulberries and stared at them dispassionately. There was nothing fierce about her.

Psyche found herself laughing despite herself.

She climbed on the donkey without needing assistance and when Erik climbed behind her, she immediately began to wonder if she had made a mistake. The closeness of his distinctly male body behind hers made her fully aware of the thin fabric between them. He picked up the rope indifferently however, without so much as an inappropriate brush, and nonchalantly urged Juno onward.

Juno did turn out to be a stout ride. She was slow and brayed much when an occupational hazard came her way, but she always got through the toughest ravines.

They rode in silence for a while.

"You, too, have wandered a bit far from home," Erik pointed out after she pointed to another direction on the trail.

"Indeed. It is a lesson to me to be more careful. But, I also needed to get away for a bit."

"From?"

She thought of the men crowding her father's library. The intimacy of the tiny donkey made it so that his face was only inches away from her and she could feel the steady beating of his heart against her back. She found herself leaning against it, then thought it must be her imagination but perhaps the heartbeat quickened a bit when she did this.

"From... life," she said, because she didn't want him to know her troubles.

As if sensing her reluctance, he did not press. "Say no more."

But suddenly she did want to say more. She did not know why but the kindness of his voice, the understanding of it made her want to share everything. It was not as if she was ever going to see him again, so what did it matter?

"My parents mean well. I know they want what is best for me. But I don't even know what that is… so how could they?"

"Surely you must have some idea of what you want."

"How can I when I've not seen it myself? I've only read about it."

"And what is that?"

"Love!" she responded almost immediately, then bit her lip, regretting her impulsive answer. "You must think me so childish."

"No, not at all."

He cleared his throat. "But, I do think that word is rather ambiguous. It means so many different things to different people."

"Ambiguous? I'm surprised you say that. I'm sure Aphrodite and Eros would disagree with you. It is no more ambiguous than war, or death, truth, or discord."

"I would argue that all those things are also rather ambiguous. But love especially so. It is such a personal thing. Each individual experiences it differently, I would imagine. Many have felt it multiple times and each time, differently."

"You sound like one of those people," Psyche found herself teasing, but her companion did not laugh.

"What does it mean for you?"

The earnestness of his voice sobered her.

"Oh, I don't know. I imagine it to be one of the most powerful feelings in the world. Something that can shake the entire universe, as pure as the first snow, as warm as a winter hearth, as powerful as Zeus's lightning bolts. I imagine it to be the source of some of the greatest and noblest acts of which a mortal is capable. A feeling that can lift anyone, even the lowest, most humble person, to the height of the gods. I don't know where I get my notions. Lucius, a friend of mine, would call me blasphemous. I'm sorry if I offended you."

Erik seemed to think for a while and when he spoke, his voice was soft.

"No. No, you have not. Love can be all those things you mentioned. But, it can also result in tragedy and death. Wars and destruction."

"So can a knife," Psyche protested. "The same knife that cuts food and feeds a family can also be used to kill someone. Love is powerful but needs to be used with wisdom and felt with deep understanding."

"How old are you?" His voice was suddenly very light again. "You could not be more than eighteen summers."

"I will be eighteen by the next new moon."

"Where did you get all these ideas?"

"The papyri of course. But, to be honest, they are not in the papyri either. Not like the way I described. The poets seem to agree with you that love is more a cause of evil and mischief and that Eros is simply a blind never-do-well."

"Hmm. It's a good thing he is probably too busy to read such papyri."

"He should. It might inspire him to use his arrows with more care."

Erik shifted uncomfortably. "Or perhaps those papyri you read would not be very interesting if they contained a healthy form of love. There would be no conflict, no betrayal, no suicide."

"Oh dear, who likes suicide? Although, you are right, they make the most beautiful poems!"

"You like poems about suicide, do you? Hades would be pleased to have your favor."

"One would be mad to favor Hades! Although, I shouldn't be so harsh. Hades plays such an important role for us."

"How so?"

"He reminds us of the briefness of life and the importance of appreciating every single moment as we may never have them again."

Erik laughed softly, and impulsively found himself touching her hair. Psyche caught her breath and was afraid to move lest he remove his hand. She knew the touch was inappropriate, but its tenderness was the most affection she had received in years and her body tingled the way it had when she dipped into the cool pond.

When Juno hit another bumpy area, Erik put his hand down, but tightened his hold around her to her keep her from falling. This change in position, however, proved even more effective, for now she could lean her head back against his shoulder while those tantalizing fingers caressed her waist and belly, pretending to be there out of necessity.

She was not being maidenly. Her mother would have been horrified, but here, in the privacy of these magical woods, discussing intimate thoughts on love, life, and death, Psyche did not care about consequences.

But Erik held himself back. For whatever reason, he removed his hand from her waist. She straightened, wondering at the rejection, but then he asked her another question.

"Do you have a suitor who might inspire some of these feelings?"

Psyche sighed, trying to hide her disappointment. "No. Not yet."

"What is it that you are looking for?"

Psyche smiled, for this was something other men had asked her, eager to think of ways to become the exact description she revealed. For a short man, she said she liked tall. For a tall man, she said she preferred short. For a musician, she declared she despised music and for a hunter, she told him music was her life. Now, as Erik posed the question to her, she thought carefully about her answer.

"I want a man who is not afraid of the world. I want a man who knows who he is and where he is going. A man with a purpose and a passion for life. I want a man who is not afraid to stand up for what he believes in, to me or to anyone; to Zeus himself if it has to be!" She thought of Lucius. "I also dislike blind stubbornness. If someone poses a reasonable argument, he would not be rigid simply because he can't be wrong." She felt like she was missing some important traits. "He also must be kind, of course. And like children. And reading! I wouldn't mind if he were pleasing to the eyes, for I'll have to look at him often. And rich, or else I will never hear the end of it from my mother."

"And does he fly as well?"

Psyche smiled, realizing how silly she must have sounded. He must think she was ridiculous.

"Only if I ask him to."

Her companion chuckled. Then sighed. "That's quite a list. I don't know if man or god can match your standards."

Perhaps this was all she needed to discourage all her suitors and make them think her standards too high. Maybe they were.

When did that happen?

Psyche sighed, lost in her thoughts of this imaginary lover. "Perhaps all I want is a man who loves me."

"Is that such a difficult thing?"

Psyche paused, contemplating the question, thinking about her mother and her sisters, finally her father. "It shouldn't be, but I find that it is. Men speak much of love and write many verses, but in the end, all they see is your face and nothing else."

"Well, you do not make it very easy."

"How do you mean?"

"You've a face that shames the moon and all the stars and can drive anyone to distraction."

Psyche seemed surprised by the unexpected compliment. She turned, "And you?"

"What about me?"

"You are not ugly. Do you worry women would not love you for yourself?"

Erik seemed to consider this. "It is not my face that I fear will lure the wrong type of woman."

"Then what?"

"My wealth and power."

She burst out laughing and he allowed himself to enjoy its gorgeous sound. Juno brayed with irritation, emphasizing Erik's depressing poverty.

"Yes, that must give you endless trouble."

"You know what you should do?"

"What is that?"

"You should disguise yourself as a hideous old woman and see who will love you then! Only the truest of hearts will stand by you."

"Yes, but what if I am not attracted to him?"

"Ah, now who is only interested in a face?"

Psyche laughed, surprised at herself. "You are right, I am no better than my suitors. But in a way, I've already disguised myself. I was quite a homely girl but a year ago. No man would look twice at me. And certainly none of them loved me."

"Ah, so perhaps, deep inside, you are paying them back for being so blind."

"No. I don't think so. At least, I certainly hope not! You have given me much to think about."

When they were finally out of the woods, Eros reluctantly descended, knowing that it would be inappropriate if anyone saw them riding together with her cradled in his arms. She was becoming more and more unbearable. Her beauty had been uncanny, otherworldly, but it was nothing to her intelligence, her humor, and her spirit. He felt as if they were increasing the poison of his arrows, feeding the unquenchable heat. This had been a mistake. He would never be able to forget the sound of her voice, the smell of her hair. And her words, her brilliant words were turning his world upside down. How could he bear to be away from her?

They did not speak until they reached the corner of a hill and she could see her house not too far in the distance. He made a move to continue, but she stopped.

"You can leave me here." She climbed off the donkey without his assistance.

"Ah, I see." Eros was glad that she was finally admitting some of her true colors to him. Her mortal colors, at least.

She did not miss the dryness in his tone.

"What is it that you see?"

"I am just a poor shepherd. It would be unseemly for you to be seen with someone like me."

Her cheeks reddened with chagrin and she looked intensely back at him.

"Clearly you have taken my jokes to heart and think ill of me. Allow me to clarify myself. I have no problem with your position in life. I am leaving you here because I want to spare you the rudeness of my mother and sister. They would not take kindly to you and I couldn't bear someone who has been so kind to me be treated badly in return."

Eros said nothing, only stared at her. Her eyes softened as he continued to gaze. He imagined what it would be like to lie on a grassy field with her, to touch her until those eyes smoldered like green fire.

As if reading his thoughts, a slow flush crept to her cheeks, and she looked away.

"You will be on your way, I suppose, to see more of the world?"

Something in her voice made him think she would go with him if he asked, and for a moment, he imagined what it would be like to live like a mortal, to feel what they felt, the urgency of the moment, the fear of death, the intensity of love, and the terror of it being lost. He imagined turning away from his duties and simply having her by his side. Perhaps finding a little pasture and tending sheep. He could continue the ruse until she... he wouldn't let himself finish the thought.

What utter and complete madness! This must end and it must end now.

"Yes. We will most likely not see each other again," Eros heard his voice catch on his throat and feared she heard it. What a weak fool she must think him.

Psyche continued to gaze. For a moment, he feared she would touch him, do something to make his will come crashing to the ground like Apollo's chariot being driven by Phaeton.

Instead, she smiled solemnly. "I will think of you when I read tragic love poems."

The sweetness of the words and the liquid warmth of her voice made him happy despite the sorrow of his heart. Even she knew it could never be. Perhaps it was because she thought him a shepherd. Perhaps because she, too, was afraid of the current between them. She was mortal, after all.

"That would be a great honor."

Psyche did not know why, but she felt like weeping. There was something so raw about him, so full of a longing she had seen in other men, but it was matched with a restraint she could not understand. Why was he holding back? Then, there was the sadness. Beneath all the merriment of his blue eyes, the teasing and the joy, there was a loneliness. How she wanted to fill it, so that he could smile forever for her, and shoot star beams into her heart every day.

Psyche wanted to do something, to let him know that he was not the only one. To make real the magic that was only whispering in the air. She wanted to say something, or to touch him in some way, but she did not know how. A part of her hoped he would make some initial move.

He did not.

She waited a second more, then turned away before his silence could sting her pride anymore. She managed to whisper a goodbye, and hurried down the hill with tears that she wouldn't let fall, all but blinding her eyes.

# Chapter 6

Eros felt nothing like a god. He could not believe how far he had lowered himself. He was sprawled in the most degrading position, peering through a miserable crack in the wall hiding behind a stack of hay and two smelly cows, watching as a parade of men waited for Psyche to enter the warm room within.

Psyche's suitors all ranged in shape and size. Few were handsome, many were old, but the room sparkled with jewelry and armor and whatever flashy attire they could afford. There were about fifty, crushed in a small room and all spoke of nothing but the beauty that was Psyche.

Eros was unimpressed.

None of these men seemed worthy of her. Had they seen her as she was that morning, in all her naked glory, they would truly have something to be agog about. Even now, the image burned in his mind. He could feel himself shiver with ridiculous excitement at the memory.

Her mother arrived at the entryway with a flourish and read a tasteless poem about beauty and divinity and finally, Psyche arrived from the hall.

For a moment, Eros could not see her, but he heard the gasp inside the room. When she finally came into his line of vision, Eros wondered if someone had stolen his arrows and just shot five more straight into his heart. If she was an elusive, natural beauty this morning, she was a surreal creature this evening and he knew it was not his poison arrow clouding his judgment. These men, these mortal, inconsequential men, knew what they were wagging their tongues about. For all their pettiness, they had an eye for beauty and impeccable quality. Perhaps that is why Olympian gods and goddesses held their opinions in so high esteem.

Psyche stood in a dress spun of gold, every bit as lovely as his mother, Aphrodite, and in his eyes, Eros suddenly did believe she was more so. Her mortality only added to her perfection, for she had a hint of uncertainty about her, even as she moved so gracefully, so fluidly. Eros suddenly realized that the room had become deafeningly silent and Psyche's eyes widened with alarm and fear. It

60

took him a moment to realize what had so displeased her, for he could barely take his eyes off her form. When he did, he thought for a moment that the whole room had cleared, but when he looked towards the floor, he saw that all the men were bowing. It was not just a bow of courtesy, as would befit even the most highly exalted members of royalty.

The men were prostrate, the deepest, most respectful of bows, on their knees, as if they were before a holy shrine.

"Can you believe this!" cried Aphrodite as she looked upon her All-Seeing fountain where the glassy reflection of the pool revealed a room full of devotees bowing before their mortal goddess. She was talking to Ares, the god of war, who was polishing his sword meditatively. "Who does she think she is? How they make such idiots of themselves!"

Ares did not even look up from his task. He was concentrating on the bloodlust that was reflecting upon his sword, excited about the battle that was to take place in a little kingdom named Troy.

"I don't know why you concern yourself so. She will grow old and die in a few years as it is. And all these swooning men will forget her soon enough."

"Not," Aphrodite seethed, "if they immortalize her in her memory. Not if she chooses a rich and pampering husband who keeps her fresh and healthy and beautiful. And look how she carries herself with that... air! No mortal woman should be allowed to walk like that!"

"I did not realize that we had made it a sin to walk. Zeus has gone a bit loose in the head if he's agreed to that."

Aphrodite ignored the jest. She could not even enjoy the way the light from the window gleamed against Ares's perfect masculine form. Normally, the chiseled outline of his muscles made her long to trace her fingers against them. But Aphrodite was too angry to pay attention to such things now even though they rarely had a chance to be alone together. Her husband by arranged marriage, Hephaestus, the god of blacksmithing, was often home and ill. Today, however, her husband was preoccupied with work, slaving away to make Zeus extra thunderbolts. She was not looking forward to having him home with his grotesque limp and the terrible smell of burnt metal all over him.

"She is not even attractive! Not in the typical sense anyhow. She looks as dark as a farm slave! Come and tell me if you see the appeal!"

Ares reluctantly peeled his eyes away from battle that was reflecting on his sword to look at the body of the most breathtaking goddess in the world beneath her almost translucent gown. His reaction was a spontaneous one. No man could look upon Aphrodite and not feel instant lust. Unfortunately, she was not in the mood for forbidden frolicking and Ares was not in the mood to chase.

The god of war swaggered slowly towards the object of his desire, touched her waist from behind, and kissed her immaculate neck. "I have eyes for only one beautiful woman," he cooed with a low, almost growling gentleness.

Any other day, Aphrodite would have responded favorably to this approach, but tonight, she brushed him away. "Just look."

Ares looked upon the reflection and his eyes immediately widened. "That is she?" he leaned forward, suddenly forgetting the sultry goddess before him with her indecent white silks.

Aphrodite stood in quiet fury, determined not to get angry until she was certain of his honest reaction.

"Oh my..." He breathed. There was something about the woman in the pool, her regal air, something about the tones of her skin and the strength of her jaw bone, the athleticism of her body that immediately appealed to Ares. He thought she looked as he should have looked if he were born a woman, as much the perfect reflection of feminine beauty as he was of male. She had his skin tone, but hers was sultry, and although her movements were graceful, there was something also very primitive, almost savage about them, as if she were restless, a gazelle trapped in a cage. He wanted to free her instantly.

There was a sudden loud clattering sound and Ares looked up to see that Aphrodite had kicked his sword across the room, destroying a nearby statue of a water nymph. "Get out!" She shouted. "Get out of my house this instant!"

"Beloved…"

"I said, get out!"

Ares knew better than to try to reason with Aphrodite when she in a fury. And he was more than a little angry that she had dared treat his beloved sword so carelessly. Ares reached out and the sword instantly flew to his hand from where it had been flung across the room. Goddess or no, he was not accustomed to such treatment. Any other day, he may have challenged her and she would have liked it, but today, he was too annoyed.

"Watch yourself, goddess. I am not one of your mortal men you can trifle with."

With that low growl, he stalked away.

Aphrodite found her anger for Ares dissipate and her fury at Psyche double. Now look what she had done! Psyche had caused a rift with her and the only man she had ever loved! It meant nothing to her that she and Ares were often quarreling and that theirs was an impossible relationship. She looked back down at the reflection of the beautiful maid and slapped the water impatiently, causing the ripples to shatter the flawless face.

"Where is that foolish son of mine? Why hasn't he done anything yet?"

Eros was doing something. He was armed with lead black arrows and shooting any man whom Psyche seemed to like. Lead arrows, the exact opposite of his love arrows, caused instant repulsion in the person struck.

If any man made Psyche smile, Eros struck him with a lead arrow and instantly he fell out of love for her. Her suitors were never quite repulsed by her, still admiring her beauty, but wanting only platonic friendship. The fact that this was the strongest reaction his lead arrows could bring showed just how passionate the men's attraction for Psyche had been.

The conversation in the room started to change. The suitors were still very much full of praise for Psyche, but all seemed to agree that no one would be good enough for her.

"My villa is not worthy of her," acknowledged a red bearded man.

"Indeed, one would spend all ones time beating the men away."

"Her beauty is far too distracting. I could never get any work done," said another wealthy merchant.

Psyche did not seem troubled by this change of event, if anything, she seemed to be enjoying the evening more. One man even started talking to her about another woman who lived across the road from him who did not seem to care for him at all.

Psyche found herself offering advice.

"Well, what does she like to do?"

"Do? Well, the activities that all women like, I suppose."

"There is no such thing as an activity all women like because women are different. You must discover what she likes. Listen carefully to her, and then surprise her with a special gift. A few lines of poetry wouldn't hurt, either. She is bound to notice you then. It may be difficult to compete with some men in strength, looks, and wealth. These are things many of us have little control over. But a man who listens to a woman best will always be a threat to all other suitors."

Eros smiled, his admiration for Psyche increasing. She was right, he knew, as he had wooed many women by simply giving them his undivided attention. He pondered what sort of gift he could bestow her. A bow and arrow, perhaps, of a quality she could only dream of, that could travel a distance that her eyes could not even decipher. Would this win her love?

Having shot almost everyone in the room with a lead arrow by now, Eros was satisfied with how the evening was progressing. None of the men posed a threat and he was getting to learn more and more about this lovely maid. He was struggling to find a way to make his appearance and enjoy Psyche's company for himself when a hush fell through the crowd.

He heard Psyche's sister clearing her throat. "Prince Lagan of Domici," she squealed.

Eros frowned and returned to his hiding spot, peering into the crack.

Prince Lagan was a slim man of average stature, with a regal air, and a trim little beard that looked almost painted on his face. He was clearly the youngest man in the room. Eros did not care for his dress, however, which included an ostentatious scarlet cape and gold studded sandals.

He looked about the room with obvious distaste. Psyche's mother, for the first time, looked small and timid as she approached him with a gracious bow. "Prince Lagan, what an honor it is for you to come to our most humble home."

There was a pause as he assessed the shrinking little woman. A slow, condescending smile crossed his face. "But, of course. I was just passing by and I could not resist the urge to see the woman who is rumored to be the most beautiful maiden alive."

"I am sure you will not be disappointed, Your Highness. Had Paris met Psyche before Helen, there would be no war in Troy. She stands before you, right over there, next to Lord Flavius."

The men in the room parted to give Prince Lagan a clearer view of Psyche who now stood up, surprised by her new arrival and impressed, no doubt, by the air of authority and wealth he carried.

Eros was already poised for defense. Here was the man Psyche had described to him during their donkey ride. A man who knew who he was and where he was going. Eros reached for another lead arrow only to grasp air. He had run out.

The change in Prince Lagan was instantaneous.

It was clear that he had not expected the rumors to be true, and Eros almost felt sorry for him. His own face must not have been so different when he had first seen Psyche by the pool.

The prince walked forward as if in a spell. Psyche had the misfortune of sitting on a platform with a trellis decorated with roses that her mother had arranged to create a greater sensation. She looked like she was standing on an altar and the goddess-like effect had been accomplished. The prince looked up at what he imagined to be his future princess with utter reverence.

"You... you are more beautiful than in my dreams."

Eros felt his heart sinking. Already, the fool was in love and he did not even need to be struck by an arrow.

Psyche, however, did not look impressed.

"You must have some very interesting dreams, Prince Lagan."

The Prince blinked and Eros couldn't stop himself from chuckling. The few men close enough to hear the chuckle began laughing softly themselves.

"Indeed," Lagan was still too entranced to notice the joke. "They have been filled with nothing but you!"

"Your Highness, that's hardly flattering—."

"Call me Lagan, I beg you."

"Prince Lagan, if you please, I don't think it is appropriate for you to judge me before you have even spoken with me. A man of true character would like a woman of substance, not just beauty, as should a woman like a man for the same. Come sit here, by the fire, and we can have a proper conversation. I'm sure Lord Flavius would not mind if you join us so that I can better acquaint myself with my mother's new friend."

Lord Flavius politely raised himself and the prince replaced him in the seat, never taking his eyes off the maiden before him.

Eros was disappointed. Psyche's impertinence did not seem to lessen her appeal to the prince and Eros kicked himself for not saving at least one arrow. One thing he knew, the prince would not get any help from Eros's love arrows of which he had a full quiver. His arrows of love could ignite passion or enhance an infatuation that was already there. If he hit any of the men in the room while they gazed at Psyche, they would be driven by madness with love for her. However, love could of course ignite without Eros's arrows. It was rare but possible. In these cases, Eros knew, the love was inevitable, designed by the Fates and not controlled by any god.

Eros slumped against the wall, feeling defeated. Still, he could not pull himself away. He watched all night for the dreaded moment Psyche's heart would fall for this perfect prince.

# Chapter 7

Mount Olympus was not its usual beatific place as hectic creatures of the sky gathered to listen to Zeus, the leader of all the gods, speak for the annual Closing of the Harvest celebration. Beneath the city, rain poured onto the earth from thick black clouds. Thunder and lightning disguised the noisy merriment of the heavens.

Eros glided to the left of his mother who lounged with unconscious eroticism on a floating chaise only three places left of mighty Zeus himself. Apollo was leaning from his parked phaeton, restless to continue his daily journey across the world. Black-haired Artemis, goddess of the moon and Apollo's wan twin, yawned sleepily not far behind him. Athena stood straight and tall next to Hera in her most formal, regal attire, her golden helmet with scarlet plumes tucked under her shapely arm. Then there was Hera, Zeus's wife and queen, unearthly beauty with hair as dark as a midnight sky and sunlight glittering like stars against it.

Eros scrutinized her carefully.

She was one of the most ancient of the gods, though her face was smooth and immaculate, round and almost childlike. If Eros's activities were to be noticed, it would be by her, for she was one of the few who had the ability to hear thoughts at great distances if she so wished, and she tended to catch the small deeds of the lesser gods, as she had a lot of free time. Fortunately, most of her energy was spent spying on her husband whose adulterous ways caused her endless misery. Now, she sat on her throne by Zeus's side, her expression never changing. Presently, she was eyeing Ganymede, a beautiful youth who was offering the gods wine for drink, but again, it was impossible to tell if she was admiring him or hating him. The goddess who could read everyone was the most difficult of all to read.

Hermes was darting above the throne keeping an eye out for danger, for to have so many of the world's deities in one small area was always a risky endeavor.

Another clap of lightning brought all the gods and demi-gods to attention, but Eros tensed for a different reason. He worried about the men and women beneath them, and the cold and misery the wet must be bringing them. He hoped that somewhere, his beloved was warm and safe.

Perhaps it was with Prince Lagan with whom she was warming herself. Eros grit his teeth, hoping this ceremony would end soon so he could return to her side.

Zeus stood proudly from his throne, his cloudy beard wafting with the light breeze in contrast with his tan, youthful skin. Unlike Hera, whose dark eyes held abysmal mystery, Zeus's eyes remained celestial, light, full of endless optimism. He created awe and inspiration by doing nothing but standing, a big smile upon his face, and a warm twinkle in his blue gaze. His kinsmen, who loved him despite the grief he often gave, surrounded him. He was their hero, their savior, the one who rescued them from the savagery of the Titans, and he could do no wrong. Poseidon and Hades, his two brothers, were not present, but they watched from afar, unable to leave their world even for such an event. They were the exception, however, and as Zeus's brothers, were allowed some leniency. Others would be punished for missing such an event, but few ever wanted to. Zeus's ceremonies were often grand and merry affairs.

Zeus spoke in a surprisingly temperate voice, given the formality of the occasion. He spoke of his joy at seeing all of his family together again, and his eyes reflected the affection of a proud father. But those who knew him best also knew he could change as quickly as the harmless lightning bolts that rested in a celestial box by his throne.

Eros shifted uncomfortably.

Did any of the gods know about Psyche? Surely they had more important things to focus on like the siege of Troy. Besides, although All-Seeing Eyes could see mortal activities, most were hard of hearing. Except for the four most powerful deities, Zeus, Hades, Poseidon, and Hera, the other eight Olympians had to be close to hear someone else's thoughts. Even then, they had to apply immense focus and concentration. Hermes was the only god Eros knew who could read a person's thoughts without looking at their eyes. As long as the room was quiet, Hermes could read them. If the room was busy, it was difficult for any god to listen, and if one kept their thoughts under control, then there was nothing to decipher. In a place like this, with so much activity and so many conversations, there was no worry for Eros.

"How is that business with Psyche going?"

Eros jumped, not expecting his mother to speak in the middle of Zeus's speech. He pretended not to hear her when she nudged him.

"Oh well, I am still waiting to get her at the right moment. The stunt with the boar did not quite work. I've been shooting her suitors with lead arrows so that they will not fall in love with her. I figured I'd wait to make her fall in love with an inappropriate man instead. I have been watching for one."

Aphrodite gasped with pleasure at the idea. "Yes, how perfect! Make him cruel, one who beats her every night of her life and wipes that smug little smile off her face."

Eros grit his teeth and forced his mind to become empty on the slim chance she might want to read them. Aphrodite's back was turned towards him, however, and she was only giving him half her attention for the other half was staring at Ares who stood a bit farther away, his glistening pectorals dominating most of his form.

Eros knew that he could not let his mother know about his attraction to Psyche. Although Aphrodite was capable of crueler deeds than Zeus himself, she was his mother. It would be worst betrayal. Aphrodite had to protect Eros often from the wrath of other gods. Many years ago Dionysus, god of wine, accused him of using his arrows on him. In front of all the gods, Aphrodite made Eros shoot her with an arrow of love while she looked at a Cyclops. When she felt no attraction, she claimed that it was proof that Eros's arrows were harmless unless the deity was weak of mind.

Dionysus did leave Eros alone after that as did the other gods. None wanted to acknowledge that they were "weak of mind." When Eros was alone with his mother again, she told him to remember what she did for him. And that there was no love more pure than a mother's love. That night, in the secrecy of her palace, she had a servant transform himself into a Cyclops and used him for her pleasure.

It was a harsh lesson to learn and Eros accepted the ways of the gods. There was always some stratagem happening, a constant struggle for favoritism and more power from Zeus. All hidden behind benign smiles. Eros learned to detach himself, and immerse himself more in the world of the humans whom he could not help admiring for their simplicity and at times, their innocence. Now, he felt himself with yet another reason to feel further isolated from the gods.

After Zeus finished his speech and the sky dancing began, Eros stole away from the revelries. He knew that few would notice he had left. He glided towards an empty palace courtyard where a shimmering fountain glistened with sparkling silver fire. For the first time in several hours, he allowed his thoughts to wander freely, to recall the shape of Psyche's eyes, and the perfection of her smile. He recalled their conversation and let the memory of her laughter seep its way into his dulled heart, pumping it hard with blood and warmth.

"I can't believe I'd ever live to see the day," a voice came from behind him.

Eros swung around to see Hermes leaning against a balustrade.

"Eros is in love," he chimed.

"Hermes, it is rude to read a friend's mind!" He said sharply, and immediately filled his thoughts with visions of Hermes screaming in a fiery pit.

"Oh, come now! That is not very original. Besides, you know chains could never hold me and I'd escape that pit in no time at all."

"They're unbreakable chains, the ones that hold Prometheus!"

"Fair enough, fair enough. I promise, I only glimpsed your thoughts just for a second. You were the one who came to this quiet little place. You made it too easy. Anyhow, who is the lucky girl? Will Olympus be expecting another wedding soon? We could sure use some joy around here. I could write a new song just for the occasion! I'll even include a tidbit about her musical laughter. Let's see:

"Alas, is that a tinkling bell
Oh no, it's just a maiden from hell

She brought the heart of Hearts to quell
And threaten a friend who's been nothing but true
With pits of fire and questionable goo."

Eros could not repress his smile. "You are a fool."

"The god of foolery! Not my best work, but give me the date and I'll have it done before your nuptials, for sure!"

"Please, keep it down. There is to be no wedding and I pray I never hear you finish that song." Eros peered closely at his friend's suspiciously bright eyes and shook his head. "Hermes, I don't know how you could have swallowed so much wine between the end of Zeus's speech and now."

"I am a god. I have my ways. If it weren't such a depressing day, I would not have let myself go so easily."

"I take it then, that the war has not abated?"

Hermes sighed, running a hand through his already disheveled dark hair. "No, not yet. Bloody Greeks are still hammering away at that stupid horse. But, it should be finished soon. And then it will be over. Yet, there is no real victor at the end of war, not with so many good men dead and buried. But that's grim talk." Hermes touched his neck as if it hurt. "What about you, I would much rather hear a love story than a war tragedy."

Knowing that Hermes would not rest without some information, Eros began very carefully, concentrating on controlling his thoughts. "It is not that romantic, I'm afraid. The female in question is… unsuitable for marriage."

"Ah, I see. But then again, women, they only seem to become more attractive when they are forbidden."

"Is that so?"

"Oh yes, I have much experience in such matters."

Eros knew it was better to keep Hermes talking than to divulge information himself. "So… what is your suggestion?"

"Are you asking me for advice? The god of love asking me about sweet amour! Ah, I have risen in the ranks, I have. Truth be told, you need only to spend more time with the girl, not less. Enjoy her, make sure she enjoys it, too. Soon, I guarantee it, you will become bored with her. You will discover that she is silly, uncouth,

71

and unintelligent. Most are. I mean, compared to a god, of course. And, since you say she is not marriageable, she cannot be a goddess."

"You sound like a man of experience."

"Indeed. I was with a nymph for almost a year. Considered making her my bride. Then I simply realized she was too petty. Too demanding. Prone to jealousy, and it was quite tiresome. There was no mystery to her, no challenge."

"It wasn't quite fair that you could read her mind."

"And what a vacant lot I found in there! Besides, anyone with intelligence could hide things from me. You'll discover it soon enough, my friend. No one woman could truly fulfill a god. Look at Zeus. He has the most perfect and beautiful of all women, Hera, and still he goes womanizing. It is how we gods are built. Love, in that silly, obsessive, and depressingly loyal form is reserved for mortals."

"I see what you're saying. You think that if I spend time with her, I will get over her."

"Precisely! You'll grow tired of her soon enough."

"So what happened to this nymph, after you grew tired of her?"

"She moved on. Oh, she protested and made quite a show with tears and threats of suicide, but no sooner did we part ways was she flirting with that demi-god of riffraff, Narcissus. The two were perfect for each other. What a close escape I made. Women are a fickle lot. Their affections are easily won and just as easily lost."

"Just like you?"

Hermes smiled with defeat. "Defending the weak are we? I am not attacking your maiden, I don't mean to offend. It is not their fault, you see. Compared to gods, they offer so little. See for yourself. Woo this girl, nymph or mortal. You are sure to find disappointment. And with it, the end to your infatuation."

"Is that what you call it? Infatuation?"

"You are the god of love and you do not even know the meaning of your power. I think this exercise will be good for you."

With a clap upon his shoulder, Hermes left the young god by the fountain, deep in thoughts he respectfully refused to read.

As the days went by, Eros watched in agony, waiting for the right moment to show himself, but it never seemed to come. Psyche and Prince Lagan were spending almost every day together.

He knew he should be happy for her for finding an appropriate man who could lift her to a station worthy of her. A reasonable Eros should accept this happy outcome and focus on saving his own hide. He should be dreaming up a good way to explain to his mother why Psyche was not only still alive, but thriving and happy, and about to be elevated to royalty.

Instead, he gathered as many lead arrows as he could and followed the pair wherever they went.

Prince Lagan, unlike him, was mortal, and capable of that — how did Hermes phrase it—"depressingly loyal" form of love. Hermes did not know what he was talking about, Eros was certain. Eros couldn't fathom ever tiring of Psyche. Yet, wasn't that the essence of love? Didn't it render one completely blind?

The idea of spending more time with the maid was hardly repulsive and if it had the chance to relieve him of his longing, then surely it was worth a try.

During a romantic evening ride on a chaise, Prince Lagan leaned over to kiss Psyche on the cheek. Eros struck him with a lead arrow and suddenly, the prince was more interested in the giant buck that had crossed their path than Psyche's smiles. However, unlike his arrows of love, Eros's lead arrows were only a temporary diversion. They wore off with time, and sure enough, when they did, the Prince was back at Psyche's side.

Eros had considered striking Psyche with the arrows, but he could not bring himself to do it. If the Prince won her heart, surely he deserved her. Still, he never saw her give Prince Lagan that look she had given him, or at least Erik, on the hill. Eros clung to the hope that she was still not in love.

Then one day, he saw it. She had dropped something and Prince Lagan bent to pick it up. He ended up losing his balance and falling gracelessly on his head. Eros enjoyed the scene as if he had caused the accident himself. Psyche giggled as she reached out to help the embarrassed prince.

Then she did a shocking thing.

She stretched her hand out and pushed a lock of hair from his face the way a woman might a fallen child. The affection in the gesture made Eros feel like he had been stabbed in the heart.

Prince Lagan, however, was too humiliated to notice and brushed her hand away and called out to a servant to get the chaise immediately.

Something had to be done.

But Eros did not know what. Hermes had said to spend more time with her, but even if he did, how could he compete with a prince? At least, how could Erik compete? Erik, as Psyche knew him, was as poor as a beggar. She had most likely already forgotten him by now. And as for Eros the god, well, of course no Prince or King or Emperor could compete with that, but he did not want Psyche to love him simply because she was afraid of him or even in awe of his powers. He wanted her love the way only mortals could love one another, not as Hermes described it, but as she had said that one day swaying back and forth on his donkey. Eros couldn't remember a happier moment in his life.

Could that have been only a few days ago? It felt like a lifetime.

What had she described? Love, pure as the first snow, warm as a winter hearth, more powerful than lightening.

That was what he wanted, too.

# Chapter 8

Psyche was again in the woods, but this time, she was with her father. After such a strong storm the day before, the trails were treacherous but exciting. It was good to be in nature with only a single purpose, to catch the largest stag in the forest. One thing she did not want to think about was Prince Lagan.

Psyche did not know what it was about the prince that bothered her. He was kind, attentive, even heroic at times. He was strong, masculine, confident. She did not feel alarmed or distrustful of him and marriage would provide her with comforts she could only imagine. He read much and mentioned that he was fond of children. But he did not laugh often, perhaps that was the problem. He took things very literally, and although he was not a stupid man, he was not particularly interesting.

But what a foolish thought, to have the only complaint be that he was too dull! In fact, if she had to be honest, Prince Lagan fulfilled each of her requirements of the perfect husband. He was the ideal that made Erik tell her she had unreasonably high standards.

Except Prince Lagan couldn't fly.

Psyche smiled at the memory of their conversation. How she wished she could talk to Erik again, perhaps even ask his advice. Even though she hardly knew him, she remembered feeling a sense of worldliness when she was with him. He would know what she should do. Perhaps, he would even suggest a wicked alternative.

Psyche blushed when she remembered the tingling sensation she got when Erik's body was pressed so close to hers on the donkey. Guiltily she looked to see that her father was still bent down, frowning over the deep tracks of what looked to be a huge stag. He had not noticed her suddenly flushing face.

For the hundredth time that day, she tried to stop thinking of Erik. It was wrong to think of another man when she was being courted by a sweet and unsuspecting prince. Psyche remembered a conversation with her mother the night before that filled her with more shame.

"Prince Lagan is an impressive man," Hermena declared as she brushed Psyche's hair.

"He is fine," Psyche looked at her hands, unable to speak her mind. Psyche didn't know what it was about her mother that made it difficult to be honest. In any other company, she could look a person in the eye and tell them her feelings, even if it might cause displeasure. With Hermena, it was impossible. Deep inside, Psyche still felt like a child who wanted to please her mother.

Hermena's eyes narrowed in the mirror. "Well, what is wrong with him?"

"I didn't say anything was wrong with him."

"Don't talk to me like I'm a fool, Psyche. I can hear it in your voice. What is your issue with Prince Lagan?"

Psyche knew there was no escaping those sharp eyes. She looked away. "I don't know. Nothing, I suppose. I just—."

"That's right, absolutely nothing is wrong with him. The only thing that's wrong is you. Do you not know that all the clothing and jewelry we've purchased are from borrowed funds? You are to marry quickly and well or this whole family will be in ruins."

"I did not ask for any of those things," she protested. "I had no need for them."

At that, her mother yanked at her hair furiously with the brush.

"You have no idea how the world works, do you? You read all those papyri and know absolutely nothing. You should be so grateful to have parents who work so hard to keep a roof over your head. What a waste to have such beauty in such a stupid girl! I should show you the type of men some women have to marry and you will go screaming to your prince sure enough."

"Maybe he doesn't even like you at all," Claudia pointed out, brushing her own hair. "Maybe he is just enjoying his time with you but in the end, he will decide you are too poor to marry."

"Nonsense!" her mother scoffed.

"He hasn't asked her yet," Claudia insisted. "He hasn't even broached the subject to Papa."

"He is merely biding his time."

"No, she is right," Psyche admitted, remembering the hot and cold meetings she had with him. It was as if he was holding himself back. His was drawn to her, but he was not yet convinced of her worth. Perhaps he was right. What was she except a momentarily attractive farmer's daughter? She had no money, nothing of great value to offer him except her beauty, and that, as all knew, would fade in time.

"He has not asked me. Perhaps he is losing interest." If there was a hint of hopefulness in Psyche's voice, it was lost on her mother.

"If that is the case," her mother said simply, lowering the drape of her neckline to an almost indecent level. "Then you must make sure you get it back."

Today, Psyche refused to think about any of it. Today, she was simply hunting with her father. She could forget about her mother's ploys, the hot and cold prince, the mean looks her sister and many village women often gave her, the cruel whispers beneath covered hands, all of it. She was simply enjoying the cool autumn air and the wondrous freedom of a short tunic again.

She looked at her father who was tracking the buck carefully with sure, determined strides. She gazed upon the back of his balding head affectionately. She missed spending time with him.

"Father, can I ask you a question?"

"Anything, my dear." He had not taken his eyes off the path.

"Do you think I should marry Prince Lagan?"

There was a bit of a pause, one that stretched for so long that she did not think her father heard the question. Finally, without stopping, he replied, "Well, that all depends."

"On what, father?"

"On whether you love him or not."

Psyche smiled, not surprised by this romantic answer.

"But, does love really matter?"

The old man stopped and turned to look at his favorite daughter. His eyes held deep affection but also a resigned sadness that Psyche had never noticed before. "You have been spending too much time with your mother."

It was the closest thing to an insult Psyche had ever heard her father say of her mother. Her father could never bear to have a word spoken against his wife. It was a loyalty that exasperated her often, even as a small part of her respected it.

"She says we are in difficult times financially," she continued. "And that an advantageous marriage is the only thing that could save us."

At this, he raised his eyebrow. "Did she truly say such a thing?"

Psyche nodded.

Her father turned and continued walking. "Utter nonsense. The day I sell any of my daughters to the highest bidder is the day I can no longer call myself a man."

Psyche's heart burst with affection, but her joy was short lived. Her father, often stuck for hours with his nose stuck in papyri or out in the forest hunting, was not often aware of what was going on with his finances. The entire family had witnessed him getting swindled at the market at one time or another. As a result, Hermena no longer allowed him to purchase anything. With Psyche's mother controlling the purse strings, there was no way her father would know if she was leading the family into financial ruin.

Her father stopped so abruptly that Psyche almost ran into him. She followed his gaze and spied the buck they had been tracking for hours. Her father signaled for her to take position at the other side of the clearing. Psyche moved away from her father with practiced silence and crept stealthily around the grazing animal.

What a magnificent creature it was! Eight beautiful points stood on perfect balance at the top of its head like the branches of an ancient tree. There was no mark on its perfect skin, as if no arrow had even been able to graze it.

As the buck chewed meditatively on the young green shoots in a small meadow, Psyche noticed a strange intelligence in the animal's eyes.

She could see her father crouching behind the brush across from her. She saw him give her a slow signal with his hand. Reluctantly, she notched her arrow. There was something about this animal that made Psyche want to leave it in peace. But before she could scare it away, her father's arrow sliced into the air and buried itself into the deer's rump. It gave an agonized cry that made the birds flap away in alarm.

Knowing that a merciful death was the only option for this animal now, Psyche stood up and aimed for its heart. The buck spied her, but instead of running away, it charged straight towards her. Psyche had a clear shot, and she knew that if she didn't kill it, it would try to kill her.

Still, she couldn't bring herself to release her arrow.

Moments later, the antlers found its way into her belly and Psyche felt herself being thrown up into the air, then landing hard on nearby shrubs. Catching her breath, Psyche looked up to see the buck about to trample her.

Psyche buried her head under her arms, bracing herself for impact. How ironic that all her worrying would be for nothing. Death would solve all her problems.

When she did not feel angry hooves on top of her, Psyche slowly opened her eyes and looked around. The only thing she saw was the bloody rump of the buck racing away behind her.

It had jumped over her.

Her father was by her side immediately, his face flushed with excitement. She told him she was fine. He promised her that he would avenge her.

"No father, let it go."

"But you know it will only suffer if I don't finish it. I will be right back after I bring it down."

Before she could stop him, her father squeezed her shoulder encouragingly, and raced after the furious animal.

Psyche couldn't really blame him. It was the madness of the hunt. She had seen her father succumb to it often. She knew he would come back for her.

Still shaken, Psyche took a deep breath. She tried to lift herself up with the aid of a tree. The pain in her ankle was severe and she could only hop a few yards before it became unbearable.

It wasn't long before she heard someone up the path, whistling a jaunty tune.

She looked up, hating her vulnerability, yet knowing that her only hope lay in getting help.

Then she wondered if the pain had caused a hallucination.

Looking quite huge and ridiculous on top of his tiny donkey Juno, was the man she had not been able to get out of her mind for weeks.

A look of surprise that matched hers crossed Erik's face when he saw her. He signaled Juno to stop.

"If it isn't the beautiful Psyche. Once more, I have the pleasure!" He dismounted and carefully tethered his mount. Seeing her leaning against a tree, he hurried towards her. "You are hurt!"

"Just a small sprain. Nothing to fret about. Indeed, I must be well favored by the gods. They always seem to bring you to my rescue."

He smiled enigmatically. How she missed his smile!

"Perhaps, some of them."

He was next to her immediately and she noticed that he was wearing the same clothes she had first seen him in before and smelled wonderfully of fresh leaves and grass.

It was amazing, the effect this illiterate shepherd had upon her. She wondered why she could never feel this way for Prince Lagan. Perhaps it was the easy manner in which he carried himself. Perhaps it was because his merry blue eyes always seemed to be laughing, as if he knew some secret joke that no one else could understand. Whatever it was, he still made her heart flap like a fish caught in a net.

"Come, let me help you to my gallant stallion."

Psyche laughed, bubbling with both humor and joy at seeing him again. She took a step towards the donkey and winced.

"Wait, give me a moment."

Before she could catch her breath, he moved forward and lifted her up. She gasped, reeling from his unexpected closeness and the feel of his hands upon her bare legs. Finally, she settled and allowed herself to enjoy being carried.

"Juno does not at all look happy to see me."

"Nonsense. Juno is ecstatic! A face like that could not lie."

The donkey looked up blankly from the wild daisies she was eating and sniffed.

He set her up carefully upon his donkey. For a moment, he just stood there looking up at Psyche. She felt a moment of uncertainty as she wondered what it was he saw.

Eros was drinking her in. The donkey she sat upon did not do her any justice, and yet, she looked as beautiful upon it as she would have looked on a godly throne.

Suddenly, Eros realized what it was that made her so uniquely beautiful. She could make a lowly donkey elegant just by sitting upon it.

What had Claudius, the man who exchanged fists with Lucius, said? She makes me proud to be mortal. Eros suddenly knew what he meant. Instead of making the environment seem paltry in her immaculate presence the way Aphrodite often did, Psyche's beauty accentuated the loveliness of her surroundings, allowing it to complement her. The green of her eyes were matching the green of the leaves that shaded them, and the beautiful multiple colors of her hair brought out the fascinating texture of Juno's furry rump. The entire world looked more beautiful because she was there.

"What is it?" The mortal asked him self-consciously.

He sometimes forgot that she could see him and it made him nervous and excited at the same time, forgetting to disguise his feelings.

"Nothing," he lied, not for the first time and not for the last time that day. "I am simply very glad to see you again."

The smile spread to her eyes, a special smile he had worried she would never bestow to him again. "As am I."

Most donkeys could not have tolerated the weight. But, Juno was not a true donkey. She was a beautiful phoenix in disguise, Eros's favorite pet. She could glide far above the sun at speeds that gave Apollo apoplexy. She could reach the ends of the earth in seconds. Her real name was also not Juno, but Lumina, but then, Psyche did not have to know this.

Eros settled in behind her and immediately felt as if his life was complete. That he needed only this afternoon, this donkey, and this beautiful woman leaning contentedly against him.

"I am going to take you straight to your house this time. And I will hear no argument from you."

"I was not going to argue."

They rode in silence for a bit as Eros contented himself with the repeat of the happiest moment of his life.

At last, she broke the silence. "So what brings you back to these woods? I was quite certain our paths wouldn't cross again."

"I am in no particular rush to leave, and as you know, my father has given me the opportunity to travel on my own for a bit."

"How wonderful of him."

"Yes, but I'm afraid he had very little choice in the matter. I would have done so with or without his permission. Also, and I'm sorry if this troubles you, I lingered longer in the hope I might see you again."

Psyche felt her face burn with pleasure and shyly looked away.

"Have you read any interesting poems recently?" He asked, recalling what she had said when they had first parted.

"I have! It truly is a shame that I cannot share them with you."

"Surely you have memorized a few lines."

She shook her head, "I could never do them justice. There is a rhythm, a precision that could only be read in order to be truly appreciated."

"Then perhaps you could teach me."

Psyche caught her breath. What a truly wonderful idea. "Teach you to read? Really?"

"I don't see why not. My father will be very pleased if I return with such a handy skill. Of course, I understand if you don't have the time."

"Oh, I will make the time. I can't imagine a more worthy cause. It will open such a world for you, Erik, I know it!"

Her enthusiasm exhilarated him. He was only looking for an excuse to spend more time with her and she was making it so wonderfully easy.

She suddenly gasped. "Oh look! The mulberries have ripened."

Juno stopped on her tracks to munch on them. Psyche reached up to take some for herself, causing her lips to stain a delectable purple. Eros couldn't stop staring.

"Ah yes, the recent change."

"Recent?"

Eros cleared his throat. It was a slip of the tongue. The change had occurred perhaps hundreds of years ago, but in the lifetime of a god, that was recent. "Have you not heard the story, in all your readings? I heard a ballad not too long ago. I may not have read as many books as you, but many musicians seem to know much about the origin of things. I can try to sing it for you if you like."

Psyche urged him, so Eros began a familiar song that Hermes had written long ago.

"Oh listen children to a tale,
In a kingdom so long ago.
Never was there a tale so sorry,
Never a lad and lady so full of woe
As that of Sir Pyramus and his Thisbe…"

Pyramus and Thisbe, two lovers forbidden to see each other because of feuding families, planned to run away together and meet beneath a mulberry tree. Thisbe arrived first but saw a mountain lion and fled. In her haste, she dropped her cloak on the ground. The mountain lion chewed the fabric to bits, then left. When Pyramus arrived, he saw the cloak and immediately thought the lion had killed her. He stabbed himself in the heart with his knife just as Thisbe was returning. When she saw her dying lover, she took the same knife and followed him to the Underworld. Their blood mingled and seeped into the ground. The roots of the mulberry tree absorbed it. As a result, the colors of its berries changed from white to red.

By the time he was finished with his song, Psyche was in tears. "Oh, that truly is a tragic one!"

"Dual suicides. I thought you might like it. But, I seem to have been mistaken. I did not mean to make you weep," he stopped, instantly remorseful. He did not expect such a strong woman to come to tears so quickly. "I hope you'll forgive me."

"No, no, they are just tears. It is not me who lost true love."

Eros lifted his hand and wiped the amazing dampness from her eyes. He was surprised how warm they were.

Tears were unfamiliar to him. The gods rarely wept, for if their emotions ever became so intense, destructive things could happen that could alter the entire shape of the universe. Yet, this young mortal wept so easily to nothing more than a song, and the effect it had on his heart was devastating.

He wanted to kiss her. Her eyes were dark green pools of feelings that he wanted to fall into. What is it about this human that had such an effect on him? Why was she such a rich mixture of strength, vitality, and vulnerability, a blanket with complicated textures he wanted to wrap himself around.

Suddenly Juno jerked forward and Eros turned and focused on keeping them both astride. He was glad of it. He did not think he could recover from such a kiss.

They had reached the bottom of the hill and were now turning towards her cottage.

Eros got off the donkey and hesitated. "It is not too late," he murmured, looking up at her. "I could still drop you off right here."

Psyche swallowed. She was afraid of her mother's reaction, but at the sight of his soft, vulnerable eyes, she found courage. "You would not make me walk all that way by myself, would you?"

The smile that spread across his face made Psyche feel warm and gave her more strength for the meeting ahead.

Clicking his tongue, Eros urged Juno on.

# Chapter 9

Psyche should not have worried. Erik had no trouble handling her mother. He explained the situation and told Hermena that he was happy to be of service to such a lovely lady. He had charm, humility, and a guilelessness that won over the ladies of the house. He was not inappropriate nor did he pay more attention to Psyche than to anyone else in the room. This was quite assuring to her mother, for it was clear that he did not feel worthy of a woman like Psyche, or anyone in the house for that matter, handsome or no.

Psyche, however, found herself wondering more about her companion. He was flattering to both ladies, knowing just what to say, smiling with a mixture of respect and allure. He complimented Claudia on her weaving and her mother on her hair. Within moments, both women were showing him various crafts they had been working on. It would appear that no one was immune to Erik's charm and it made Psyche feel less special. Perhaps collecting the adoration of women was simply a happy past time for someone like Erik.

Just as Psyche was starting to feel less and less important, Erik's gaze captured hers and they exchanged an intimate look that made her feel silly for ever doubting.

When Psyche's father returned home, his face was haggard and his words remorseful. He was not able to find the buck. It was as if it had disappeared into thin air. When he returned to see Psyche gone, he was terrified. He apologized to Psyche for leaving her alone and thanked Erik profusely for helping his daughter. After insisting that Erik return later to join them for dinner, Hermena protested.

"He cannot stay!" cried her mother. "Prince Lagan is coming."

"Why should Prince Lagan care if we have another guest? Yesterday, Lord Flavius was here and you did not object."

"Lord Flavius is…" she was about to say, 'not threatening' but then, that would be silly. Surely Lord Flavius who owned acres of land and at least thirty slaves would be more of a threat than this… sheepherder's son. But still, there was something devilishly charming about young Erik.

Hermena looked at their guest up and down as an idea formed in her mind. Perhaps, it was just the thing Prince Lagan needed. A healthy sense of jealousy that would push him to finally ask for her daughter's hand.

"You are right. It is the least we could do for this young lad bringing our precious Psyche back to us in one piece. Please, return just after sundown, Erik. We will be so pleased to have you dine with us."

As Psyche walked Erik back to Juno who was happily munching on her mother's geraniums, she felt his silence and the barrier that was widening between them.

"Prince Lagan of Domini?"

Psyche opened her mouth but found that she did not know what to say. "You've heard of him?"

"I have. My father would sometimes stop by his lands to sell some wool. You have done quite well."

"Please don't say that."

"I was not chastising you."

"Yes, you were."

"I insist, I wasn't. I would not have wanted you to have anyone less worthy for a suitor. I am actually quite surprised that the King of Sparta is not knocking upon your door right now claiming that he has promptly forgotten all about Helen and wishes to have you instead. I would not recommend him for a spouse, though. He seems to have a slightly jealous streak."

Psyche laughed.

She had been complimented many times, in many ways, but Erik's joking manner always took her aback and made her feel so differently, so much more special. Perhaps it was because she could never truly read him. Perhaps it was because although he was so kind to everyone, he always made her feel like they shared a secret.

Erik then pulled out something from his pocket, and placed it in her hand closing it so that she could not see what it was. "Unfortunately, ours would not be a blessed union. Allow me to feel for you the way a brother might feel for his sister, if you would give me that honor. I have rescued you enough times from peril to make me feel a bit protective. I would like to meet this prince of yours tonight and determine, for myself, whether or not he is worthy of your attention."

"And if he is?"

"Then I will bid you farewell and a happy life."

"And if he isn't?"

Eros smiled a mysteriously. "Then I will snatch you away forever."

As if realizing what he just said, he swallowed and backed away. "Let us hope he is worthy."

"Let us hope he is not."

Eros did not seem to know how to respond, but Psyche smiled grimly and broke her gaze as color burned her cheeks. Could she truly love him in this attire, with dirt streaking his cheek and the smell of donkey and manure clinging to his rags?

"For the sake of what is in your hand, let us hope that he is."

Hermena appeared near the doorway and Psyche hastened her farewell.

"Of course," Psyche broke her gaze. "We shall see you at dinner."

He bowed his head courteously, released her hand, then stalked away. Psyche leaned against the door watching him go. It wasn't until he was riding in the distance that she looked down and opened her fist.

In them were some crushed purple mulberries, its purple juices staining her palm like an ominous warning.

Angrily, Psyche threw the berries to the ground and turned away from the door.

The dinner was awkward, as expected, but Erik showed no sign that he was affected by it. He was the perfect guest, asking cordial questions but not dominating the conversation.

Prince Lagan was appropriately condescending. He had never in his life broken bread with such unworthy people. However, when he discovered that Psyche had made the food, he insisted it was absolutely the best he'd ever had.

"The best food I've ever had was in the island off the coast of Carthage," Erik offered.

"You have been to Carthage?" Prince Lagan's tone suggested he deeply doubted this.

"Yes, but only once. My father insisted I learn the language of the sheep over there. It was rumored that there was a man who could talk to animals the way a human would talk to another human. If one learned this skill, one would have powers immeasurable."

Prince Lagan failed to suppress a derisive sound. "For a sheepherder, no doubt."

Erik smiled beguilingly, and bowed in humble agreement. "Indeed. Anything more would be overstepping ones true place in life."

"Do you truly believe that, Erik?" Psyche protested. "Do you truly believe that you could be no more than what people expect of you?"

Her passion was evident and Erik proceeded cautiously, weighing his words. "I believe that there is a proper order to things and that to move away from that order is to go against nature."

"I agree," Prince Lagan interjected almost begrudgingly. "There is nothing more repugnant than someone who tries to rise above their station in life. Can a fish really live amongst the eagles? Or a worm become a bird? It may want to, but it is not meant to be."

"You're analogy does not quite fit the subject at hand," Psyche replied more sharply than she intended. "I am not asking a fish to become an eagle, I am suggesting that a man with the potential to become a truly great man should be allowed to do so. Is not our religion inundated with stories of people who come from humble beginnings only to raise themselves to the level of the gods through merit? Did not Hercules, a mere mortal, become a god? Did not Pygmalion eventually turn his statue into a flesh and blood woman?"

"Only by the grace of Aphrodite," Lagan retorted.

"And doesn't Aphrodite favor the pious, the pure of heart, the truly deserving?"

Erik coughed and had to take another drink. Nobody seemed to notice as the girl across from him raged on.

"Pygmalion was a talented, devout, and loving man. Aphrodite honored him because he represented purity of heart.

Doesn't that suggest that people have a right to happiness if they are worthy and deserving?"

"Happiness," Erik repeated thoughtfully. "Now that is a different topic. Had you asked me if I wanted to be happy, I would have said, 'Certainly.' But we were talking about social climbing. I am but a humble herder of sheep. It may not seem like much to those in this room, but I am quite proud of my work. My animals are treated well and as a result, they honor me with good wool and meat. They harm no one and I harm no one. It is a peaceful and happy life. I do not think Princes have it much better."

Lagan laughed at this, but he lifted his wine cup to the man across the table. "A noble speech. I salute your philosophy, friend. I wish there were more good men like you."

Psyche, however, was fuming. "More men like him? Men without ambition? Without the desire for challenge, to do more than what others believe them capable of doing? A useless lot we all would be if that were the case! What is the point in anything if we all become herders? I am not belittling your occupation. For any other man I would have embraced your speech, believed your happiness in your work, and wish you all the best. But you are not any other man. You are bright, and brave, and strong and so intelligent! You have an inquisitive mind and a quick wit, and you have the manners fit for a court of kings. It is an unjust hand that placed you at such a position in life. A wasteful hand!"

There was a shocked silence after Psyche's passionate speech. Upon realizing what she just said, she blushed profusely. She reached out abruptly for another sip of wine, wondering if she could use the brew later as an excuse for her embarrassing words.

Erik spoke slowly, carefully weighing his words with his audience. He wasn't sure he trusted his voice. "I am quite touched that you have such an opinion of me."

"Clearly it was a false opinion," she responded, placing her wine down more firmly than she intended. "Apparently, I do not know you at all." She stabbed at the meat, refusing to look back up at him.

Erik looked clearly wounded by this. Before he could say anything, Psyche's father interjected.

"I do not see what is so wrong about being a sheep herder. It sounds to me that it could be quite tricky work, especially going all the way to Carthage to talk to the man-animal. His intelligence does not seem to be wasted on that."

"Indeed, not," Erik agreed carefully. Psyche was out for blood and he had become quite wary of her.

"So really, it all has worked out quite well for you." Psyche's father smiled gently and Eros immediately knew where she had gotten her warmth.

"My father," Prince Lagan surprised everyone by breaking the silence, "was the second son and did not get the throne even though he was a stronger and more favored leader. When his older brother died in a tragic chariot accident without an heir, my father was instantly given the crown. I am only a fifth son, so there is little hope of my obtaining the throne, but my family's gain had been the will of the gods. It was not done by any willful deed of man."

"Prince Lagan," Psyche began in a tone that made Erik feel sorry for the man. "If you are so against social climbers, then what does that make me? I am not of royal blood. I am in fact, quite penniless and the daughter of very simple farmers. How could you believe what you believe and have any notions of wanting any attachment to me? I must be nothing more than amusing sport for the likes of you and your kind."

"Psyche!" Her mother cried out.

Prince Lagan paled considerably and Eros was sure he was going to get up and walk out the door. He suddenly did not want this. He would feel responsible for ruining Psyche's only chance at happiness.

"That is one way of looking at it," said Erik quite smoothly. "It might appear that a good but humble family like Psyche's has much to gain from such an advantageous marriage. But, as Prince Lagan pointed out, the gods favored his family. He inherited his fortune after the death of a kinsman. Perhaps our Psyche is also much favored by the gods who gave her unearthly beauty not just in face and body, but in mind and character as well. Add to this a bright spirit, unwavering courage and an intelligence that would challenge any educated man or woman of royal blood.... or any immortal for that matter." This last part, Eros suddenly realized was also true. It shook him. Yet, he forced himself to finish the speech. "It would seem that the gods positioned her to make her a worthy match for princes and kings alike. In which case, it is Prince Lagan, fifth in line for a crown, who would be honored to have a woman fit to be a goddess for his wife."

Silence rattled through the table as the revelation of his words sank into the minds of the listeners.

"I concur," Prince Lagan broke the silence with a large smile, relieved that such an answer existed so that he would not be forced to leave the table. "I could not have said it better myself. That is exactly why I stay!"

Psyche did not respond. Her heart was beating rapidly. She had never in her life felt more beautiful.

Unfortunately, the compliments did not come from the man who should have spoken them. It did not come from the man she was allowed to love.

# Chapter 10

A banquet was held the following evening to celebrate Psyche's eighteenth year. Psyche and her suitors, and after much insistence, Erik, had been invited. He was not much welcomed, however, and few of Psyche's guests deemed him worthy enough to speak to.

Many assumed he was a servant and he had to correct them, especially when they handed him their empty cups expectantly. After the third cup, however, Eros resigned himself to picking them up. It was easier than trying to explain to people who seemed to enjoy the sound of their own voice over anyone else's. Eros caught Prince Lagan's eye as he held a tray of empty cups. Prince Lagan's eyes rested on him, then slowly and deliberately, looked away without acknowledgement. Eros tried not to wince. Still, it was not too different from Olympus, only somewhat more ridiculous. The organization of mortal deference seemed far less to do with true strength and power and more to do with the appearance of it.

How he wished Lord Flavius would do away with his diamond rings and studded clasps. Every time the older man moved his hands, the glare gave Eros a slight migraine.

When Psyche finally managed to greet him, she touched his arm and smiled warmly.

"I am so glad you have come," but before he could respond, another suitor began a conversation and led her away from him.

Still, the simple words and the intimacy of her tone made it so that Eros no longer minded picking up the cups of the men who were deemed more important than he, at least in this form. It was definitely a test in humility. He wanted to show her that he would be willing to survive any insult just to be near her.

In fact, he mused, she would never know to what actual degree. For a god to be playing the role of servant to mortal men... ah, if only Hermes could see him now! He knew Hermes would chew the wings off his shoe at the blasphemy.

When Psyche finally saw what Erik was doing, she immediately took a cup from his hand. "No, no Lord Flavius, Erik is not a servant! You mustn't—"

"It is fine, Psyche," Erik murmured.

"It is not fine! Why do you keep letting people—"

"A song, what a wonderful idea!" Psyche's mother suddenly appeared and grasped her arm. "Claudia go fetch Psyche's lyre. Go on now, you know where it is in the closets. Psyche, get ready now."

"No. Mother, I haven't played in years."

"I told him you had a voice that would make Hermes swoon."

"But that is far from the truth."

Hermena grasped her upper arm, a warning in her eyes. "Then make it the truth. It was Prince Lagan's request." A little drunk herself, she swayed and released Psyche's arm before moving away.

Looking at Psyche's stricken face, Erik smiled encouragingly.

"Don't worry," Erik consoled her. "It will come back to you and you will play wonderfully."

Claudia appeared with the lyre and set the instrument upon the stage somewhat smugly. She was looking forward to seeing Psyche fail at something at last.

"I don't know any songs."

"Of course you do. You know all those love ballads."

"Erik, you don't understand, I don't know how to play."

The panic in Psyche's eyes made Eros realize that she was more petrified than ever of singing in public.

Making a quick decision, he climbed up the crude platform that sufficed as a stage and stared at the sea of mostly male faces. He bowed elegantly, making the audience take a second look at the bedraggled figure before them.

"Ladies and gentleman. At the special request of the esteemed Prince Lagan who has travelled all the way from the mountains of Domini to be with us tonight, we shall enjoy a beautiful ballad sung by the magnificent Psyche of Seventh Hill."

Immediately, there was applause. Knowing she had no other choice, Psyche climbed the stage next to Erik and curtsied much less gracefully.

She was surprised when Erik picked up the lyre and looked at the instrument in confusion. It looked old and unwanted. He plucked a string only to make a horrendous sound and jumped with exaggerated surprise, making the audience laugh.

"I do believe this instrument is older than my grandfather. In fact… I believe this instrument is older than Lord Flavius who, I'm certain, remembers breaking bread with the Titans."

The laughter was especially louder this time and included a good-natured chuckle from Lord Flavius who was clearly the oldest man in the room.

"'Tis no matter, all it needs is the soft breath of a beautiful woman. Is there any such woman in the room?"

"Of course there is."

"She is right next to you, man!"

"You must be daft!"

Erik looked confused, then turned to look at Psyche. "This one?"

The audience cheered their approval and Erik smiled at Psyche next to him. He presented the old instrument before her with both hands. "A puff of air, my lady."

Psyche gave him a dubious look, but blew softly.

Other than a little bit of dust that flew up, the instrument looked unaffected.

Erik played another note, and it sounded worse than the first. He tugged at his ear as if in pain, bringing out more amused laughter from the men.

"One more puff, my beautiful lady. This time with passion, with spirit, with energy! Pray to the god of Hermes that music may be enjoyed this very night. Let's give her some encouragement!"

The cheer was deafening and Psyche couldn't help but laugh at their exuberance. She turned back to Erik who seemed quite at home being the showman. She marveled at the different talents he seemed to be hiding beneath his rags.

"Now, on the count of three. One… two…"

At 'three', Psyche blew as hard as she could. A puff of dust covered her sight. She coughed softly as the audience, the stage, and

Erik himself temporarily disappeared. She had a surreal moment when she thought the whole world had disappeared.

Eventually, the cloud faded and she waved the rest of the dust away only to see that the lyre in Erik's hand glittered like new. When the dust settled and everyone could see the instrument, there was at first dumbfounded amazement. Then someone in the distance began clapping. Soon the whole room was thundering with applause.

"He's a magician!"

"Amazing!"

"How did he do that?"

"That is one clever slave!"

Erik moved away and began plucking the lyre, now beautifully in tune and making sounds of the like that Psyche had never heard before. He began playing a song whose melody she recognized immediately as the song of Pyramus and Thisbe that he had sung to her the other day.

Psyche immediately began humming the tune and received the most beautiful smile from Erik that gave her courage even as it weakened her knees. Erik began the familiar song and soon she recalled the simple lyrics. With Erik's prompting, they both began to sing, at first, her line an echo of his lines.

"Oh listen children to a tale, in a kingdom so long ago
Never was there a tale so sorry,
Never a lad and lady so full of woe
As that of Sir Pyramus and his Thisbe…"

Once there were two houses standing,
With a wall of stone cut between,
But the wall might well have been built
As wide as the River Styx, as wide as the River Styx."

The chorus was easy to remember, and after a few more lines, Psyche was able to sing in harmony with Erik. Soon, there was not a single dry eye in the room. Even Psyche could barely sing the last lines,

"As the water where two rivers meet,
The blood of two loves combine,
That of she and that of he,
On the branch of the mulberry tree.
Turning red the fruits of white
Turning love the shade of night
To bleed eternally, in our hearts, in our eyes
On the branch of the mulberry tree."

After the last haunting note from Erik's lyre played, there was a silence. Everyone in the room seemed to be absorbing the sorrow of the song. An instant later, the room shook with applause.

Erik and Psyche moved forward, took each other's hand, and bowed elegantly.

Even Psyche's mother was dabbing her eyes. She leaned towards Claudia. "You see, that is what happens when children disobey their parents! No good comes of it. Pay heed, pay heed!"

A few minutes later, Psyche was in a heated debate with Lucius and her mother. "You both have it completely wrong. That is not the moral of the story at all!"

"Then what do you think is the moral of the story, Psyche?" Lucius mused with a tolerant smile.

"That families should not feud so! That a forgiving heart could save innocent young people from needless tragedy!"

"Bah, nonsense!" Her mother cried with a dismissive wave. "The song never explained what the feud was about."

"It doesn't matter what it was about," Psyche insisted.

"Of course it does," Hermena shot back. "One just doesn't go about forgiving the wrongs of one's neighbors! Where would the world be with such a philosophy?"

Lucius was rocking on his heels in amusement as Psyche fumed.

"I don't know," Psyche threw her hands in the air. "Perhaps it would be a kinder, gentler place. A place where love can thrive and doesn't have to end in horrific tragedy!"

There was a small pause. Then, Lucius and her mother laughed abrasively.

Eros moved away, sympathetic to Psyche, but unwilling to assist her in this particular debate. It was one to which he had not yet formed an opinion. But he admired her passion as well as her resilience. He watched as she pointed out historical incidences when forgiveness would have resulted in less death and carnage. As she continued, several men were starting to agree with her. Whether it was because they wanted to impress her, he did not know, but she made some convincing points. If only Zeus could hear her speak, Eros mused.

It wasn't long before he spied Claudia watching him with a look that made him uncomfortable. After a moment of hesitation, he moved towards her.

She spoke before he could greet her.

"You're not fooling me, you know."

Eros froze, surprised. For about the millionth time in his existence, he wished he had the All-Seeing eye so that he knew exactly what she meant. Instead, he had to rely on her truthfulness.

"What do you mean?"

"I don't think you're a shepherd at all."

Eros swallowed, looking about the room to make sure no one was near enough to hear them. Fortunately, everyone seemed to be fascinated by the debate.

"Then what am I?" Eros asked softly, leaning in to her ear.

"You are… a sorcerer. Just like my sister." Claudia swayed a bit, and Eros realized she was more than a little drunk.

Eros let out a slow, relieved breath. He steadied her gently, and looked at her with a quizzical smile. "Easy there, little one. Perhaps you should take a seat."

He led the tipsy girl to a quieter area of the room and took her drink from her. He smiled lightly. "You know much about sorcery, then?"

"I do. I live with a sorceress after all. Psyche has put a spell on you the way she has put a spell on everybody."

"It would appear so."

"But not me," she shook her head so vigorously that golden curls struck her chin. "Never me, you see."

"Indeed, you are clearly immune to her."

"But what is different about you is... you've put a spell on her, too."

Eros tried not to look concerned.

"And if I'm not careful," Claudia continued, "you might put a spell on all of us."

"You must try very hard to be careful then."

"Don't you fret. I will be very, very careful."

# Chapter 11

It was their first lesson, and Psyche had brought a papyrus filled with her favorite poems. She chose adventure ballads, thinking that Erik, being male, would prefer the exciting tales. But he had not been very interested, fiddling restlessly with some flower petals. He pointed to a butterfly that fluttered straight to his fingers. Psyche gasped at the sight and instantly dropped the papyrus to lean close and observe the magnificent colors of the lovely specimen.

"Just look at those wings!" She breathed, "They dazzle the eyes. How wonderful that it is not at all afraid of you."

"Hold out your hand."

She did so and to her pleasure, the butterfly perched itself upon her outstretched finger.

She gasped at its stillness.

"You really are a magician!"

A strange look came upon him, but he merely shrugged.

"Butterflies are attracted to beautiful things," he murmured.

As always, his compliments fell from his lips with an ease that amazed her. There was something about him today, she did not know what it was. He wore the same rags he always did, but his moody petulance belied his humble attire.

"Erik, tell me about your home." Psyche's gaze was still affixed to the butterfly that adorned her finger.

He looked taken aback. "What do you mean?"

"I mean where you're from, and what your family is like."

He hesitated and looked at the sun for a while. Then he sighed and fell on his back, lying on the lush grass as if it were a bed of soft cushions. Psyche yearned to lie next to him, but resisted, as she knew it would be inappropriate. Instead, she hugged her knees and looked down at him, admiring the way his hair curled against the grass and his eyelashes seemed slightly lighter at the tips.

"Not much to tell really," it was a voice she hadn't heard him use before. It was weary, almost bitter. "The same as all families."

"It cannot be as bad as mine."

"What is so bad about yours?"

"My mother. It mortifies me when she goes on and on about who owns the most lands and who rides upon the most gilded chariot. I hope you don't think too poorly of us."

"Not at all. You're family has invited me into their home, have extended their generosity to me on several occasions. And your mother, well, she has her reasons, I suppose. It must be difficult to want so many things and not being able to have them."

"Isn't that most people? But, it is definitely harder for her, I think. She used to be from an aristocratic family, you know. She won't talk about it much, but in marrying my father, she lost all of it. My father fancied himself an intellectual, a poet of sorts, but was forced to farm for a living. Had it not been for my mother, he would have lost everything long ago."

"So there you have it. There is a reason behind her actions. Had your father been ruined, you and your sisters would suffer, too. And, no princes would ever come to call."

He said it so easily that Psyche sighed and finally allowed herself to lie down next to him, convinced that there was nothing but camaraderie between them now. She wanted his advice.

"Do you think I should marry Prince Lagan?"

Erik shot up as if the grass burned him. "You ask me this?"

"Why not? You have met him, you know me, and I know you have my best interest at heart. As a brother—"

"A brother?"

"Yes, that was what you called yourself. You feel protective of me, as would a brother."

Erik ignored the comment and in a tight voice responded, "Prince Lagan will be a smart choice for you. A reasonable choice. That is what mortals are renowned for, no? Their impeccable reason."

"What do you mean? Erik, you are acting strange."

Erik immediately got up, his face veiled with a warm smile again. Psyche was beginning to notice when his smile did not completely reach his eyes.

"Bring love poems next time," Erik insisted before he left. "They are the ones I care about the most."

As he left, the butterfly on her finger fluttered away and seemed to follow him.

As promised, the next day Psyche brought scrolls of papyri filled with her favorite love poems. They sat under the shade of a cypress tree and she began reading in a steady, musical voice, the verses that were so dear to her heart. When she tried to teach him letters, he waved her away.

"I'd rather listen today."

And listen he did, without interruption. He stared out into the valley deep in thought. A few moments, she caught him looking carefully at her, a strange expression on his face. Her favorite moments were when she finished a passage and he responded with a mere, "That one was very nice." Otherwise, he would just nod and ask her for another poem.

Finished with the verses, Psyche put the papyri down and lay on her back next to him. She felt peaceful as she watched the clouds.

"Love is very important to humans," Erik murmured softly.

It was a strange comment, but Psyche shrugged. He had been acting strange ever since the banquet. Her voice was teasing, hoping to lure him out of the dark spell he seemed to be under. "Yes, we humans, unlike you shepherds, do value it, at least it would seem so based on such writings."

She closed her eyes feeling peaceful, enjoying the warmth of his skin several inches away from hers. Moody or not, she was still painfully attracted to him.

"Is love still important to you?" He asked, his eyes still closed.

She turned to look at his face. He did not stir from his position and did not look particularly curious. She answered with an equally nonchalant shrug. "Of course."

"Then, you love Prince Lagan?"

The question took her by surprise. This time, she looked at him more directly, but his eyes were closed, his countenance undisturbed.

"What a thing to ask!" She snapped at him so that he was forced to open his eyes and look back. She knew why she was annoyed, but she was startled when the same emotion appeared in his blue gaze.

"Usually when questions are asked, they are answered civilly, not shrieked." His haughty tone made her blink. He did not sound like the sweet and humble Erik she was familiar with.

He sounded like arrogant royalty.

Psyche refused to be cowed. "Not always. If the question is inappropriate, it need not be answered."

"Now, suddenly, there are such things as inappropriate questions between us."

Psyche began gathering the papyri. He had not moved and this enhanced her irritation. She wanted more from him, more of a reaction. He had been nothing but cold and aloof with her. What game was he playing at? Was he purposely trying to push her away? If so, then why did he insist on meeting with her like this?

"There is a wall between us, but it's not visible," she muttered.

"Whose fault is that?"

"Yours! You said you wanted to be like brother and sister."

"I also said I wanted to snatch you away forever."

"Words, words. Easy to say, as substantive and consistent as that cloud."

Suddenly he was holding her, clutching her arms in a grip so tight it almost hurt. "A cloud? You trifle with me? You come with me and then what? Do you think the gods will bless our union?"

"I don't see what the gods have to do with my feelings or my choices."

Eros looked at her with staunch disbelief and released her so abruptly she almost fell over. "You have such audacity."

"I don't mean to sound irreverent."

"Really?"

"I am a believer. I respect the gods. But, I know my heart. And I know... I know I have control over it."

"Is that so?"

There was hurt in his eyes, but also something else, the desire to take on the challenge perhaps? She did not know.

Suddenly, she did not want to know. She was afraid of herself. Control, what control?

"Erik, this conversation will get us nowhere."

He did not respond.

"If we cannot be civil to each other, I will bid you farewell."

"Do not go."

The softness of his voice froze her in place.

She suddenly wished his eyes would close again so that she wouldn't see her own torment reflected in them.

"Please, stop asking me such personal questions."

"Of course."

She could not bear to look at him, so she turned away.

For a moment they sat there, silently. A cloud blocked the sun and Psyche lay back on the grass, furious at her own thundering heart.

Why couldn't Erik be a prince, she thought unfairly? Could she really be happy being a shepherd's wife, worrying about whether her children would be fed? These were not thoughts that a woman in love should have. None of the poems she had just read had any such musings from tormented lovers. Love should not be so realistic, so practical.

Psyche couldn't help it. She knew the cost of falling in love with an unsuitable man. She watched as her mother's adoration for her father turned into frustration, then resentment. Her mother would never forgive her and her family would be ruined by the financial loss. What sort of alignment could her sister ever hope for when her brother-in-law was of such lowly birth? And for whom would she make such a sacrifice? A man who was too afraid to tell her what she most wanted to know?

Psyche could not even look at Erik. What was she even doing by spending more time with him? Inviting disaster?

"I must go."

She got up and hurried down the hill. She did not know if she was disappointed or relieved that he did not call her back.

# Chapter 12

The tavern was noisier than usual that evening. Eros heard the voice behind him and tried not to show alarm.

"Rumor has it," Hermes began, "that the cursed Psyche, the most beautiful woman in the world and Aphrodite's sworn nemesis, the reason why her temples have been barren for so many weeks, has indeed fallen in love with a most unsuitable man."

"Is that so?" Eros clutched his cup tightly.

"Absolutely. An illiterate shepherd's son. Only a breath above a slave. You could hear Aphrodite crowing from miles away."

"She must be very pleased."

"Oh, very pleased indeed. She says she must have the best son in all of Olympus."

Eros said nothing.

Hermes lowered his voice. "What have you gotten yourself tangled up in, boy? Is this the girl you told me about at the Harvest Ceremony? The one you asked my advice for?"

Eros did not respond.

"Forbidden fruit, indeed. No wonder she was so desirable."

Eros stirred at last. "It is not like that."

Hermes gave him a playful slap on his back. "Then it must be some kind of game you are playing! The god of love himself would not be so easily susceptible to mere mortal tail. A wager perhaps? Dionysus put you up to it! Are you to keep me from all the fun?"

Eros had enough. "Keep your voice down!"

"We are in an alehouse, Eros. No one can hear us."

Eros pushed his hand through his hair. He was in over his head and he knew it. He did not know where else to turn. "It is no game." He closed his eyes at the pained memory. How foolish he had been. Why did he open his eyes? Why did he let this happen?

"I accidentally pricked myself with my own arrow while I was aiming at her. I am an idiot and now I'm in a mess I cannot hope to be free from!"

When Hermes remained silent, Eros risked a glance up at him. They exchanged solemn looks, then Hermes let out a rich, guttural laugh that irked the god of love.

"Oh, my, how I needed that! After such a somber week and debacle with that blasted wooden horse!"

"I take it the Trojans took the bait."

"With a little help from some dream visiting, yes. Surely you could feel the agony of so much death, even without the All-Seeing Eye."

Eros shivered. He had felt it, how could he not? It was so strong it clouded his joy in being with Psyche. She tried to read him war ballads, but he could not stomach it. Not when he sensed what was going on so far away. How much he wanted to confide in her, to ask her what her thoughts were on the situation, to ask her if she thought he did wrong in helping to initiate the war. Would she hate him if she knew?

Eros took another sip of ale, wanting to numb the pain of his conscience. The room seemed to move unsteadily, and he started to wonder if he had too much ale. "Well, I'm glad my little story could amuse you."

"Oh, it did! And, I plan to get more of it. Oh Eros, how on earth could you have let this happen?"

"It wasn't my fault. It was that blasted boar."

"A boar? What does a boar have to do with it?"

When Eros explained his mother's plan, Hermes's eyes widened. "She wanted to make the girl fall in love with a wild boar? The actual animal? Aphrodite is absolutely out of her mind!"

"She thought it fitting for the sin inflicted against her."

"Well, if those arrows are strong enough to make a beautiful woman chase after a hog, then imagine what it's done to you. If the rumors are true, she must be quite a vision. But, then again… I did hear someone say that your arrows do not affect gods."

Eros gave him a look that silenced him immediately. Hermes had never seen such a dark thundercloud in his friend's face. It was quite startling, even as it relieved him. So the bright, shimmering Eros really did have a weakness! Hermes hoped he never had to use it against him.

"She is more than just a vision," Eros continued. "If only she were just that. You told me to spend more time with her, and I have, and it has not dissipated my affection in the slightest. She is certainly physically beautiful, there are very few who can compare. But, she is more than that... She is irresistibly intelligent, I feel as if I could talk to her forever. Her thoughts are not empty at all. She has a response to everything. Hermes, she is so clever! She has these amazing ideas about people and the world. Her mind is so bright and optimistic. So hopeful, but not in a vacant, naïve way, but with this strong, deep understanding. She is a fraction of my age, yet she grasps things even the oldest of gods could not. She makes Zeus's thunderbolts feel like they're striking you in the chest. She thinks in poems. She talks in verse. And when she laughs... I would give up my immortality to hear that sound for a mortal's lifetime."

"Careful..." Hermes warned, suddenly uncomfortable with the turn the conversation was taking.

Then, Hermes laughed again. The men around them turned at the sound, but did not comment.

"What is so funny?" Eros snapped.

"Ah, Love," Hermes wiped a tear, still chuckling. "It makes Hades smile and Eros weep. Who would not find pleasure in that?"

"Eros."

This only increased Hermes's mirth. He sat back on his chair, shaking his head. "A woman. A mere mortal woman. Not even a demi-god, my friend. Not even a nymph. River nymphs, I grant you, are a cut above the rest, but not even a mountain nymph. They're beautiful but a stone hard lot!"

Eros's eyed flashed warningly, but Hermes did not notice and continued, enjoying the sound of his own wit. "If she must be mortal, Fates, at least make her a princess! But alas, those old cronies have a much richer sense of humor than I ever give them credit for. I bow down to it! Eros, quite possibly the handsomest, most desired god alive, the master of love and seduction, has fallen for a farmer's offspring, one of many, I would imagine, since farmers are not known for their self-restraint in bed. The most common of peasants. A dandelion in a garden of roses. My, how standards have fallen!"

The cup in Eros's hand landed hard on the table. "She is anything but common and my standards have never been higher.

That farmer's daughter would overwhelm Athena with her wisdom, she would shame Diana with her virtue, and she would—"

Hermes's hand flew to his friend's mouth, not wanting him to say anymore that might damn him forever. But when he lowered them, Eros continued in a low hissing voice, "She would take those Golden Apples right from under my mother's nose."

Hermes sat back, sobered by this transformation. He marveled at the girl who could incite such a reaction. Arrow or no, Eros must have accidentally pricked himself several times in his occupation. He doubted it ever had this type of affect. Could Eros's arrows only be affective if combined with something else? Perhaps an intangible ingredient that not even the gods could control? He wondered if even Eros himself knew.

"Have you tried lead arrows," Hermes suddenly suggested. "Couldn't they offset the poison?"

"I have already tried that. It is useless. The lead arrows are the only ones that don't affect the gods. They hardly make a dent on humans."

"That is a shame. I've said it before, I'll say it again. We should leave humans alone to their own devices. They are trouble for all who come near them."

"I cannot. I am physically ill if I part from her. I am mad with desire when I am with her."

Hermes slapped the table with his hand. "I know the solution to your problem."

"More advice? Have you not ruined me as it is?"

"Don't blame me for this. I had no idea you were apparently in love with the pinnacle of human perfection, unlikely as that might be. But this time, I have a sure proof plan. The cure to every poor, lovesick soul."

Against his better judgment, Eros asked, "What is it?"

"Heartbreak."

Eros's eyebrow rose in question.

"She cannot be as perfect as you have painted her," Hermes continued. When Eros opened his mouth to protest, Hermes raised his hand to stop him. "Let me finish. I have no doubt she is smart and beautiful and charming, blah blah, but that does not make her divine. Divinity is a rare attribute reserved only for gods. We gods can see and feel things that no mortal is able to do."

"Obviously."

"As gods, we can spend our time, limitless time, on things most humans cannot. We enjoy art, music, philosophy. We appreciate intangible joys and value priceless virtues. We have the choice to give ourselves to higher, more important causes. Psyche does not have this freedom. She is prone to mortal weaknesses."

"I have not seen it."

"Of course you have. You are just too besotted to admit it. She's a commoner, Eros. Look around you. Look at these men. They barely have any time for themselves, they spend their lives toiling in the dirt trying to make a meager living. Commoners need to survive, to feed their families, to support their children. These are all weaknesses."

"How are those weaknesses? They make people stronger. Struggle gives people character."

"That's what we tell mortals so they don't complain! You think these mortals see value in love? They are not allowed to. They exert all their energy on basic survival, what use do they have for love? Can they eat love? Tastes rancid from what I hear. You rant and rave about giving your right arm, about giving up your *immortality*, by Zeus, and she has promised you *nothing*. Your affection is one-sided, lad. She may desire this Erik the shepherd, but not more than she loves herself. Not more than she loves creature comforts, luxuries, wealth, security, a full belly night after night. Once you see this, you'll see her for what she is. Another mortal scraping to survive. We can't blame them, it is not their fault for having to do this, it is just the way the world is."

Hermes took another sip of ale. "Loving is not wrong, Eros. But loving someone who does not love you back with equal ardor, that is foolishness. And if you're that type of fool, perhaps you ought not to be considered divine."

Despite the nonchalance of his demeanor, there was a warning in Hermes's tone. Eros rubbed his eyes wearily. He did not wish to argue today.

"Perhaps you are right. In a way, she has already rejected me."

"Really?"

"She thinks I am a shepherd's son. There are times when she does not let me get too close. It is as if she is afraid of her feelings. Furthermore, she has a handsome prince vying for her affections."

"Prince!" Hermes snorted unbecomingly and took another sip of ale. "Any mortal who bullies enough neighbors can call himself a prince."

"He is not so bad. He would treat her well and in the human world he is quite a catch! I cannot possibly compete with that."

"So there you have it. Do your really believe she would choose you, a gatherer of sheep, a trader of wool, over a grand prince? One who could give her money, wealth, power, most importantly, peace of mind. She is like every other human out there. You'll see it for yourself when she chooses this prince. You'll see the selfishness in her eyes."

"Selfishness," Eros whispered, trying to fit the word with the generous, compassionate beauty who owned his heart. He found himself shaking his head. "It is not her fault. She did not choose poverty."

"No one ever does. Have you told her how you feel about her?"

Eros shook his head. "She must know already."

"Really, Eros. You'd think I was centuries older than you as opposed to a few years. For humans, no one knows anything until it is declared. And for a woman, your love will mean nothing until you offer yourself completely to her."

Eros stared blankly at him.

"You must propose marriage."

"But... that is impossible. It's forbidden! My mother—"

"Oh, for Zeus's sake! You will not have to go through with it. She will not accept you."

Eros blinked. "She won't?"

"Eros, listen to me. A shepherd over a prince? Unless, of course, you wish to add stupidity to her long list of attributes. Do not give her more credit, those poison arrows couldn't have knocked all your sense away."

"So when she rejects me…"

"The cure to every love. I promise you that. The only way to stop a heart is to break it. You'll see. It will give you toughness like you've never known before. You will see her for what she is and you will be able to move on."

Eros studied his uncle with new eyes. Hermes was quite a handsome god even in human form as he was now, and was never in want for female attention. But there was a sadness there that he could not understand. Who was it that hurt him? One thing was certain, Eros never shot Hermes with one of his arrows. At least this heartbreak was not his fault.

Heartbreak. It was something he had never experienced before. One cannot experience it if one had never known love. Eros imagined the devastation he would feel when Psyche told him that she did not return his feelings. The pain was almost physical. Eros had thought that mortals had a greater capacity for love because their time on earth was so short. Love needed to be powerful, hurried, and desperate. But, perhaps it was the other way around. Perhaps gods really could feel it more strongly, albeit, more rarely. Eros knew in his heart he would give up everything for her if she asked. For her to not even wish to sacrifice a prince for him, a prince she may not even love….

It would make him feel like a fool.

It would devastate him, and he may never wish to see her again.

Then an idea came to Eros's mind. "What if she says 'yes'?"

"She will not say 'yes.'"

Eros was irritated by Hermes's certainty. "What if she does?"

Hermes shrugged. "Then, she would have proven herself. In a way, she would be making as much a sacrifice for love as humans are capable."

"And an equivalent sacrifice for a god would be…"

"Marriage to a human," Hermes took another sip of ale.

"Hardly a sacrifice if it means being with her."

"Not unless you break the rules and risk the wrath of Zeus. I've sat idly by long enough while you badmouth your betters. Take care, lad. Do not wish for what you know nothing of."

"I know enough about my feelings. I know life is not worth living without her." Eros took a deep breath. He had already confessed to Hermes. There was nothing else he could do now. "Thank you for your advice. I don't agree with everything you say, but you have been a friend."

"Never forget that. I am on your side here."

Eros rose wearily, wanting to believe him, wondering if he would regret this conversation. "I must go. I have much to think about."

"She will not say, 'yes', you know."

Eros smiled sadly. "I know."

"Perk up! Rejection will be the best thing that ever happened to you. You're a god. You must see the bigger picture. You'll have eternity to get over her."

At any other time, Hermes's smile would have been contagious, but today, Eros was not affected.

He was worried that eternity would simply be unbearable without her.

# Chapter 13

The next morning, Eros wasn't sure if she would come. But, when he saw her figure appear at the foot of the hill, a deep relief washed over him. He was not ready for her rejection just yet. It would have saved him much trouble, perhaps even needless pain, but such was the irrationality of love.

Without realizing it, his eyes burned with a special intensity. The unabashed warmth surprised Psyche. She returned the smile despite herself. She had been prepared for something else. The cold, aloof stranger of before, perhaps, but certainly not this raw, unfettered joy at the sight of her. It made her tingle to her toes.

"I was not sure if you would come," he greeted.

"I considered not coming," she admitted. Then added, "For about half a second."

The pleasure of his face finally overcame the sadness in her heart and Psyche allowed herself to enjoy what little time they had together.

Psyche had received news that the prince was requesting a meeting with her father. Of course, it could have been about anything, but under such circumstances and based on her mother's scuttling excitement, it could only be about one thing. She would most likely be promised soon. The little time she had with Erik, she was not going to miss, no matter how irritated she might be with him.

"Come, I wish to show you something."

His hand was outstretched.

Psyche hesitated for a moment. There was no purpose to the gesture. He was not helping her up on his donkey. He was not assisting her on difficult terrain. He simply wanted to hold her hand. The intimacy of the request struck her. She wondered if he even noticed the burning that went through her body when she touched the hand. He held it tightly however, and did not let it go throughout their walk.

The day was spent walking through the woods and pushing through the brushes. Psyche was usually quite comfortable hiking

112

through the woods, but in her long skirts, the way was more treacherous.

Fortunately, Erik was spry and attentive. When the path was a bit more uneven, he would swing her across with a speed and strength that surprised her. He did not have the burly bulk of some men, but he had no difficulty lifting her to jump across a bubbling creek or twisting ravine.

Finally, they arrived at a clearing that appeared to be the edge of a cliff. In the center was a large weeping willow that provided a shelter of draping leaves.

Psych gasped in pleasure as she entered the canopy and sighed at the flecks of sun that peaked through the branches.

"It's so beautiful!"

"Yes." He was looking only at her.

Psyche looked shyly away and sat down on a gnarled root. "Shall we begin our lessons?"

"Alpha, Beta…" He repeated the entire alphabet with ease, not yet sitting down.

Eros wondered what she would say if he told her that he did not need to read. That he could touch a book or a piece of paper and understand its entire meaning in no time at all. She seemed so excited about the prospect of teaching him. He admitted that the process somewhat fascinated him. How tricky it was for humans to get things done! Yet, he respected their determination and their patience. He respected the joy they received from the smallest accomplishments.

"Shall we read some lines?" she interrupted his thoughts innocently.

He wondered how much longer he could pretend with her.

He constantly found himself fighting the urge to tell her everything. To tell her who he really was, and ask her if she would be willing to spend her life with him.

It was a temporary urge. Eros doubted she would even believe him. He pictured her gathering her papyri and backing away slowly, making some excuse about rain and hanging laundry despite the clear skies. Then he would have to fly after her, revealing his true form, making her scream in fright and probably faint. The eyes

113

of Olympus would find them and the punishment would begin. So many rules broken, all for nothing. He would lose Psyche forever.

Eros moved closer, suddenly overwhelmed with a desire to protect her. But he pretended he did so in order to ask her a question about the papyrus in his hand.

As she answered, he found himself too distracted by her nearness to see what was written. He could see a pulse beating against her neck and a soft flush crawl to her cheeks. The intensity of his feelings made him catch his breath.

A lock of hair swept across her face and her finger carelessly touched her cheek to brush it back. Eros couldn't decide which he would have preferred to kiss more, her fingers or her cheeks.

Suddenly, her green eyes were upon him, lush fertile pastures, warm and inviting.

"Erik, you aren't paying attention," she chastised gently.

"I am paying closer attention than you know."

The blush that warmed her cheeks was too irresistible. Eros recognized it for what it was, an invitation that her mind was not ready to give but her body was offering. He leaned forward, intending simply to brush his lips against that warm cheek, but she pulled back sharply causing him to almost fall face-first into the grass.

"What are you doing?"

He straightened himself up. He was not used to rejection of any sort, from mortal or immortal. Those who did turn him down only did so to tease him, to extend the tantalizing foreplay that would inevitably lead to carnal rewards.

But Psyche's feelings were clear. There was fear in her eyes. She did not want him to touch her!

Eros decided to try again, for this fumbling schoolboy tactic was not at all representative of his talents. Was he not the god of love? Falling on his face, indeed. How Hermes would laugh!

With all the finesse he could muster, Eros took Psyche's hand gently, as if she were a frightened, wounded animal. She tugged half-heartedly, but when he held her firm, she finally allowed herself to watch breathless as he leaned forward and kissed the back of her hand.

He was not inexperienced, contrary to his earlier bumbling. He could be patient, he could control his urges. She was worth every effort. Eros softened his voice, no longer disguising the burning in his eyes.

She stared at him with unabashed longing and Eros took it for encouragement.

"I know I do not have a lot to offer."

He kissed the inside of her wrists, her thumb, the palm of her hand.

"Erik, don't do this...." She did not, however, try to pull away.

"I do not have a lot to offer," he continued, stroking her arm before planting another gentle kiss, looking up at her earnestly as he spoke.

Was it really his voice shaking? Eros never felt so nervous. Every kiss made him burn for more. Yet, he could not hurry. She was too important.

"I am but a poor shepherd."

His lips reached the inside of her elbow, an area she did not even know could be so sensitive, causing wild fire to spread from her arms to her torso.

"But, I do have my lips. They can make you laugh, sing you endless ballads, tell you stories that would entertain you for years and ... give you pleasures unimaginable." Those lips were now transitioning to her upper arms and Psyche closed her eyes, anticipating their sweet touch. His mouth barely touched her, however, though his words continued to entice areas that his lips could not reach.

"I also have my hands..." he murmured.

Psyche was suddenly aware of those large, strong hands finding their way to her ribs, not quite touching her breasts, up to her shoulders, then down her arm to entwine with her hands. Meanwhile, his lips continued their journey up her neck.

"They know how to work very hard." Was it her imagination or did it sound like his breath was labored? Psyche thought she had stopped breathing. She could no longer hold herself up. As if sensing this, he gently laid her on the grass, his lips continuing their delicate

115

exploration of her neck and her ear lobe. His hands slid down to her belly.

"These hands can do things," he breathed. "They are capable of giving you anything you want," and those hands were now at the curve of her bottom. At the same time, his lips touched an extremely sensitive part of her neck and Psyche gasped.

She felt like a woman possessed.

He was stimulating her in all directions, with his lips, with his hands, and most intensely, with his words. When those wicked hands moved from her bottom and slid all the way to her breasts, she could not fight herself any longer. She pulled at his golden hair to drag his lips to hers, but was surprised when he instead went to her cheek sending a fiery trail all the way to her chin and down her neck.

"Erik, please."

"I have my mind," he continued, gasping now against her neck, refusing to be interrupted. "It's sharp and strong like my hands. It will do its best to protect you, to stimulate you..."

Psyche was moaning heedlessly, writhing against the crushed grass. His hands were wandering and teasing in areas she rarely allowed herself to touch. She couldn't believe she was allowing it. Then she couldn't imagine how she could allow herself to stop it. She felt heat all over, and an urgency that overwhelmed her. Her eyes were sealed shut, her body tight against him, and his fingers spread her, opened her as if uncovering all her secrets. She opened her eyes and saw his face, the searing desire in them, the adoration, and she was lost.

"Sweet, beautiful Psyche," he whispered and it was the last thing she remembered him saying before he moved those fingers one more time and her body exploded. She cried out and all she saw were dazzling stars falling all around her. She clung to him, completely useless, her legs dead weights beneath her.

Several moments later, she was aware of him pushing her hair back, staring at her flushed face, glistening with spent passion. She blinked up, not certain what had just happened. Her clothes were still on and yet she was certain she had been deliciously ravished.

His lips were moving and it took her a moment to hear what was being said. She heard the word "Heart," and realized with amazement that he was continuing his speech.

"...Can withstand anything, if you would take it. Only if you would have it."

It dawned on her what he was asking. She forced herself to shake the misty fog that was filling her mind. Was he asking her to be his?

"Psyche, let me hold you like this forever. Let us never part again."

She forced herself to focus. Before she could stop him, he said, "Psyche, be my wife?"

She pulled away instantly.

"Please, Erik, say no more." She could not bear to see the anguish in his eyes so she busied herself straightening her clothes, her face burning with shame.

"Do my words offend you?"

"No. No, they are..." She looked at him then, his hair tousled, his eyes sad. Goodness, how can someone so young carry such sorrow? If only she had the power to make them smile. If only she had the freedom. "Your words are the kindest, most beautiful things anyone has ever said to me. You do not even know.... But we mustn't...."

Against her will, she began to cry.

He reached out for her, but she again, she pulled away, knowing that she did not deserve his comfort.

"Erik, I can't. I can't marry you. I'm sorry."

Psyche watched as the spark that had always been in his eyes seemed to fade and vanish. She had never hated herself so much in her life.

Even though Eros expected the answer, it hurt him nonetheless. He had tried. He had used everything he had, all the promises he could make, and he had spoken from his heart. Still, it was not enough.

Love was not enough.

"I know." He tried to sound convincing, but the bitterness had seeped through. "It's all right. I understand."

"No, you don't understand. You can't know! If it was just my decision, if it was just me, I would say, 'yes', a thousand times! But there is my mother, father, and my sister to consider. They are relying on me for so much. I cannot be so selfish. I cannot, I cannot..." and she began to weep again.

Of course, it was difficult for her. If only Psyche knew how well he understood. He had a mother, too, one who would disown him if she knew he had just asked her mortal enemy to be his wife. He had power, wealth, the heavens. All of which he would lose for her. But Psyche could not match his love. How could she, a mere mortal? He offered her everything he could think of, everything love could offer, and it was not enough.

Hermes was right. Mortals could not love as deeply as gods. At least, this one could not.

But Eros could not blame her. Psyche was mortal, designed for self-preservation, bound by fear, limited by death. How could he expect anything else from her? Yet, she was the one he wanted. The one he would cherish forever. Hermes was wrong about that. Eros's broken heart did not free him. Not when it was broken so sweetly, with such sorrow and regret.

Psyche would be a part of him forever. To remind him of all the forms love could take. Even the ones that ended could still be pure.

He pulled Psyche to him, needing her comfort as much as she needed his. This time, she accepted. He kissed her hair as she wept into his chest.

Unable to stand her tears and starting to fear his own, Eros picked up the papyrus that was crumpled next to her. He hoped to distract her, to distract himself, and dull the sorrow. He began reading, still holding her tightly,

"What is love but a momentary glimpse,
A keyhole into the depths of paradise..."

She wept more heavily.

He put the paper down helplessly and kissed her head again as if to apologize.

# Chapter 14

When Psyche awoke, she saw that Eros had fallen asleep holding her. From this proximity, she could see every curve of his perfect face, his angular jawbone, his flawless skin marred only by the dark, purple circles beneath his eyes.

She touched his face slowly, gently.

Without even thinking about it, she leaned forward and placed her lips upon his. It seemed ridiculous, after the intimacy they just shared. Yet, it was her first kiss, and the innocence of it remained, pressing against the softness of his lips. She did not know lips could be so soft.

She pulled back and saw that his eyes were half open, observing her but not moving.

Something in them sparked a wickedness within her. Suddenly determined, she moved closer and pressed her lips upon him again.

This time, he responded, softening his lips but allowing her to determine the pace of the kiss. Then finally, as if unable to stop himself, he moved forward and pressed her more closely to him.

Eros, of course, was a practiced kisser. He was aware of all the different areas, some so minute within the mouth and around the tongue that could tantalize a woman. He used his experience on Psyche but was shocked by the effect she was having on him. Her response was immediate and at first surprised him, then pleased him, then drove him to madness.

She was an incredible kisser, her inexperience compensated by natural passion and enthusiasm. She was kissing him back with such abandon, picking up his careful skills and turning it back on him. He knew her to be an innocent, but did not expect such a fast learner. She reacted as he would have dreamed her to react, raw, uninhibited, it was as if she knew exactly how to move her body, how to press herself against him.

Eros was losing his self-control. He found himself upon her, crushing her to the ground with an almost barbaric urgency. All his careful plans of wooing her trampled to the ground. He allowed himself to reach beneath her skirts and feel the softness of her skin, the heat of her. Then, he could feel the transformation occurring, his wings wanted to sprout, his disguise was falling apart. She was close to seeing him in his true form!

He pulled away from her lips and buried his face against her neck.

"We must stop," he gasped.

She was still writhing beneath him, letting out a moan that was almost his undoing.

He tried again, "Please, you must hold still."

"Erik, I don't want to stop. I don't want to think. Please..."

And she was kissing him again, begging into his mouth, and he was kissing her back. He could feel the soft outline of her breasts against the white linen of her dress and the sharp, jutting attention of her nipples against his palm. He grasped them both enhancing his tortured arousal, only to let go and slam both hands against the ground and physically lift himself off of her and roll onto his back.

"Woman, you will be the death of both of us!"

Although Psyche was disappointed that he stopped, she was also pleased by the thick passion of his voice. At least, it had not been easy for him.

She turned to her side and looked at his profile. His control intrigued her. The tense muscle of his jaw showed that he was still not in complete control. His eyes were closed and one hand was against his forehead.

When he finally turned to look at her, she had a small, slightly victorious smile upon her face.

"What are you smiling about?"

She tilted her head to one side. "You do like me."

"Ridiculous woman," he reached out for her and clutched her to his chest. "I do not know how I will breathe without you."

Psyche bit her lip, for she was beginning to wonder if she could ever breathe without him.

"But tell me, why do you trifle with me so?"

Psyche swallowed, wondering how to tell him.

"I want something from you," she declared, "to remember you by."

He kissed her hand. "A token perhaps, of my eternal affection? A handkerchief, a necklace, a ring?"

"No," and she moved forward, her hands moving through the front of his threadbare tunic more suggestively. "A memory that will last me through my old age...."

She kissed him again and he thought he would go mad with desire. But he knew it was a dangerous game they were playing.

Allowing himself to give into her would spell absolute disaster.

His disguise could only be upheld if he maintained his self-control.

After several moments of inner turmoil, he pushed her away. "You do not know what you are saying!"

"But, I do!"

She reached out for him again.

He knew he had to think of another tactic before it was too late. If Zeus knew what he was about to do, it would be the end of both of them. And if he allowed himself to succumb, if he allowed her to see him in all his glory, she would surely scream and it would be heard throughout Olympus.

Eros dropped his voice coldly.

"Then you must think so lowly of me. Is that all I'm good for? Not good enough to marry, but good enough for a quick tumble in the grass?"

Her hands fell away immediately as if he had doused her with cold water.

"No, that is not it at all." But, she knew that was exactly what she wanted.

Erik got up.

"I understand you do not think me worthy of you. But to want to use me so cruelly, knowing full well you will haunt me for the rest of my days. It is thoughtless and selfish of you. Nothing but the marriage bed deserves what you and I have with each other."

Psyche was shocked.

She had heard of women being insistent upon this fact, but never did she think a man would say such words. Her mother told her it would never be the case.

Psyche couldn't bear to look at him, embarrassed and ashamed of her feelings. She threw herself at him and he rejected her.

But then she realized what he had just said. A marriage bed. He still wanted to marry her, despite her rejection, despite her lack of decorum, her lustful nature. He was only upset because he thought she only wanted to use him.

And indeed, she had, until now.

Suddenly, she saw him, as if for the first time. A man who knew his worth, who knew his value, offering it to her completely. What was all the reading for, what was all the passion for, if she could not live the lessons they were trying to teach? Love was not something one scoffs at, or brushes aside, or sacrifices for one's parents. It was like saying, "no" to a gift from the gods. Surely her family would understand? Perhaps, in time, she could convince them. And she could try to pay her family's debts. She could help with the sheep, she could sew or earn a living teaching people how to read, and she was always clever with money. They would not be stupendously rich, but they would have love. Love. True love.

More valuable than a kingdom. Men and women have died for such a chance. And here she was, throwing it away, wanting only to molest it, to degrade it, to cheapen it.

"You are right. You are right!" She breathed. "Please, wait just a moment."

With sudden determination, Psyche looked around her and found a long blade of grass, then another, and another, then some purple wild flowers. Then, as if possessed, she began frantically weaving a crude shape.

Eros watched her, bemused, amazed at the dexterity of her fingers.

"What are you doing?"

"Just give me a moment," she insisted. She worked as fast as she could. He saw that she was creating a crude organic band, interweaving flowers and stripping pieces of grass, her fingers moving with wild speed.

Finally, she looked up from her work. Her eyes were glowing, her cheeks flushed, and her lips upturned in the sweetest of smiles as she held up the green and purple bracelet between her two fingers, triumphant and afraid at the same time.

Unable to look at his eyes any longer, she reached down and grasped his hand, easily slipping the strange ornament onto his wrists and weaving the two ends quickly together.

"A marriage bracelet," she declared. "I want you, more than I have ever wanted anything in my life. Not just for now, not just for a memory. But for as long as I live."

"Psyche…"

"Erik, you said you loved me. Others have said this, but when you say it, I believe you. With you by my side, I feel like I can do anything. Bear anything."

"But the prince. A palace. More wealth than you could ever dream—"

"Means nothing without you. Without us. Erik, you are my breath. I love you and if you love me, then that is all the treasure I need."

Erik tried to open his mouth but she stopped him with a kiss. His ears were ringing with rapture. They were the sweetest words he had ever heard and if he could believe them, then perhaps he could find a way.

But first, he had to secure her safety. He had to make sure the others did not know what he was about to do.

He pushed her away hastily, his face dark as he looked at her, as if searching for something, but she did not know what.

"If what you say is true," he said the words as if he barely believed them, "then there is much that needs to be done. We haven't any time to lose."

He rose distractedly and helped her to her feet, his mind moving quickly. "I must go for now. But you must meet me tonight. It has to be tonight."

# Chapter 15

Eros watched her go. They kissed one last time at the top of the hill, her face flushed with excitement and anticipation and her eyes held the promise of unimaginable joy. Psyche did not know that it would be the last time she would ever see her Erik.

Eros had never felt happier or more alive. He had not expected this. She wanted him. She wanted him in his worst, most unworthy form!

His heart was thundering. He couldn't believe she wanted to marry him. A poor shepherd. Such a creature who could have any man she wanted! He had never felt so special, so important in his life.

He turned to Juno still tethered to a tree. He remembered Psyche's expression when she held up the little bracelet, which still remained bound to his wrist, never to be removed, he promised himself.

The most precious ornament he had ever received.

His fingers touched its tightly woven form, his eyes beginning to glisten at the memory of her words, the sincerity of her eyes. The purity and the trust. Guilt was starting to seep into him. A voice inside him said that she still did not love him, Eros. She loved a lie.

Eros ran a hand through his hair. It didn't matter. It shouldn't matter. She loved him. He could not disappoint her. He would do everything in his power to make her happy. He would give her anything she wanted, and if what she wanted was Erik...well, Erik she must have!

Eros rode Juno deep into the forest before allowing them both to transform and shoot up into the sky. He tried to ignore the voice that kept telling him that the deception was wrong.

When Eros entered his private quarters, he was startled to see his mother lounging against one of his armchairs.

She was as exquisitely beautiful as ever, her golden hair piled above her head like mating serpents. Her white silk almost translucent gown was draped carelessly over her apparently nonchalant posture.

"Eros, my son, I have missed you these several weeks." Her voice had the melodious purr of a tigress.

"Mother, so have I," Eros cursed his own dreaded apprehension. He didn't know why his mother always had this affect on him.

"I find that hard to believe." She spoke softly, with just a touch of hurt that made Eros feel guilty and nervous at the same time.

"Mother, I have been quite busy—"

"So, I've heard."

Eros swallowed and wondered which one of his mother's countless spies may have told her about Psyche.

Even now he knew his mother was probing his mind, seeking out answers, but Eros was careful to keep his thoughts under control.

She could not interpret them without knowing the full background.

Finally giving up, she asked, "What is the progress with Psyche?"

Eros forced his heart steady. He must not allow his mother to find some other means, some other creature to take over Psyche's punishment.

"I have a plan for her."

"I thought we already had a plan."

"We did, but it did not work. My arrows have little effect on her."

This caused her to raise her eyebrow.

Aphrodite was silent and Eros knew she was trying to read his thoughts again. Desperately, Eros began thinking of another woman, a beautiful, mindless young nymph he had enjoyed a summer with, one that his mother would have found a suitable match for him. He had to fill his thoughts with something because the emptiness would have been suspicious at the very least.

"I see. And why should this be so?"

"As you know, my arrows affect men more than women, often to different degrees. She, apparently, is nearly immune."

"I have never heard of such a thing."

"Of course you have. Athena can attest to it."

"Athena!" Aphrodite almost spat. "That barbaric excuse for a woman!" Her distorted face abruptly softened and her soft, feminine cheeks returned to their usual symmetrical perfection. "Athena, for all her unworthiness, is a goddess. Certainly she may be more difficult to affect, but this creature is mortal."

Eros shrugged. "I cannot explain it, only report the results."

"Very well, what is this new plan?"

"I am the new plan."

"I beg your pardon?"

Eros walked to a statue of a water nymph reaching up towards the sun that was setting behind the mountains, watching the water splash against her in glistening waves, focusing on lascivious thoughts that would repel his mother from trying to read them.

"She is exquisite," he breathed. "Funny, how I never noticed before."

"Eros, child, focus for a moment! You can chase after nymphs after this meeting. I haven't time for this."

"Sorry mother, what were we talking about?"

"Psyche!"

"Yes, that silly girl. Well, mother, the plan is that she falls in love with a man, namely me, in the guise of a poor lowly shepherd. You probably notice that I have been spending quite a lot of time with her."

"It has come to my attention," she admitted, staring at him earnestly. His mother did not want to believe ill of him. Eros knew that he had this to his advantage.

"I would have expected nothing less." He smiled affectionately and he noticed how she responded to the smile, softening her gaze a bit. "Well, when I am done with her, she will be the laughing stock of Greece."

"Do you intend to lie with her?"

Eros forced his mind to empty, for his reaction to the idea of making love to Psyche would have caused his mother to kick him out of Olympus forever. "Can you blame me, mother? She is quite the temptress. But, don't fear. It all works to our advantage. After I'm done with her, she will be a fallen idol. Her reputation will be in tatters, by her own volition."

"You plan to break her heart? How is that worthy punishment? Innocent hearts get broken every day."

"Not just her heart, mother, her spirit. Her very soul. She will not even be able to look at herself without self-loathing. After such shame, she may be driven to any desperate act. It wouldn't be the first time that a woman kills herself over a broken heart."

"I see what you're getting at. Rejection can be a brutal punishment when done properly. But why does it have to be you?"

"Mother, who else could win her heart in a way that will drive her to such insanity? This woman's affection is as elusive as Zephyr. Nothing but the most delicate, charming, and seductive of men will be able to win her. And you are surprised I volunteered?"

Aphrodite paused for a moment, and mother and son stared at each other in a gaze so penetrating, the columns seemed to tremble.

Finally, a triumphant smile broke the goddess and she looked with deep affection at her son. "Then she is in grave danger, indeed. For who could resist the god of love?"

Eros forced his smile to reach his eyes and looked back at the statue of the lovely nymph and stroked her thigh suggestively. "Who indeed?"

His mother laughed and clapped. "Let us celebrate! We shall have dancing girls to tease and tantalize you, but no satisfaction you shall get. Oh no, you shall save that for our unfortunate little Psyche."

Eros flinched, but fortunately, his mother had turned away to give orders and was done trying to read his mind. Was this really who he had been before? Did such things really entertain him, the way his mother seemed certain they would? The idea of any other woman near him made his stomach turn, but he was no fool. His mother was still watching, and if he were to save the one he loved, he needed to put on a good show.

# Chapter 16

Psyche could barely contain her joy. She was to be Erik's at last!

It would not be easy, she was certain. Her life would have hardships, but she was a resourceful, able-bodied woman. She may not know much about sheep but she could learn. And even if they live a humble life, she could find happiness and joy being with her beloved and raising their children together.

Already she was dreaming of the tiny ones they would have together. Perhaps, he would place them on his shoulder while he worked, and in the afternoon, they would rest on the grass and talk endlessly, laugh, and play games. She could tend a farm while he worked with the sheep. They would teach their children how to hunt and track, girl or boy. She doubted Erik would have such stringent rules about the sexes as her mother had. He did not seem to mind at all that she liked wearing men's short tunics and run around in the woods.

The more she thought about her choice, the more excited she became.

Why had it taken her so long to realize?

She froze mid-step when she saw that Prince Lagan's horse was at the front of the house, his guards standing stiffly by the door. She was not in the mood to entertain him, but then, it would be best to keep her engagement a secret for now. She did not know what her parents would say or how her mother would react. Although she knew her father loved her, where her mother was concerned, her father could not be relied upon.

Prince Lagan's form appeared at the door. His stride was wide and confident as he went towards her with outstretched arms.

Psyche hesitated. Where was this boldness coming from? Then she remembered with deep trepidation. He had asked to see her father earlier.

Prince Lagan took her hands and her heart filled with dread.

"My beautiful Psyche, I am so glad you have returned at last from your walk. I have some wonderful news. I have spoken to your father and he has given his consent."

Psyche tried to pull her hand away, but the grip was firm. "His consent to what?"

"To marriage, of course."

She could not hide the displeasure on her face. Why could he not wait? Why could he not wait until after tonight when she would be safe and sound in the arms of her husband?

"But… you have not even asked me, yet."

"Well, you didn't expect me to ask you before I asked your father, did you?"

Psyche knew she had to end this right now. There was no way around it. Prince Lagan was a reasonable man and his pride should assuage his wounds in time.

She took a deep breath and looked straight into his eyes, wanting to make this as painless for him as possible.

"Prince Lagan, as honored as I am by your request, I'm afraid I cannot marry you."

The blood flooded into his cheeks.

"You… what?"

"I've already promised myself to someone else."

As confusion registered on his face, Psyche saw her mother come out of the shadows. How long had she been standing there?

"You ungrateful, wretched child!"

Her mother was upon her before Psyche could even step back. Instinctively, Prince Lagan moved to protect her, but he had not anticipated the strength of the older woman's anger. Psyche winced as she felt her mother's hands dig into her arm. The strike that landed on her cheek shocked her more than it pained her.

Hermena put her hand to her mouth and stared at Psyche with sudden remorse.

"Oh, darling, what have I done?" Psyche was suddenly pressed to her bosom in maternal affection. "I did not mean to. I'm so sorry I've hurt you. Prince Lagan, please understand, my daughter is overwhelmed by this whole situation. It was not very well done of you, you know, to approach her in such a sudden manner. Why, there wasn't even a hint of romance in it. You must give her time."

Prince Lagan, dazed by the entire incident, seemed too baffled to respond.

Psyche had managed to push her mother away. "I do not need time," she gasped, tears still streaking her face. "I will not marry him."

She saw her father appear tentatively at the door.

"She just needs time," Hermena insisted.

Unable to believe that anyone would ever reject him, Prince Lagan nodded.

"Yes, I suppose I could have been more thoughtful about it. I am not in the habit of proposing to women. I shall return in the morrow. Hopefully, all shall be righted then. I bid you farewell."

When Prince Lagan left, Psyche felt certain her mother would resume her beating of her and moved closer to her father.

Her mother approached her, her voice surprisingly mild.

"What a shock this must have been to you, my dear. I know you weren't ready for it. But you must know what an opportunity this is." She looked to her husband. "Please tell our daughter what a great opportunity this is for her."

He reached out for Psyche and clutched her hand. "You will want for nothing, my darling."

"But father, I do not love him."

"Is he not someone you could grow to love?"

"Perhaps, if I wasn't already in love with another."

"In love with another?" Her mother gasped. "Why, who on earth could you be in love with? I have pushed away all your other suitors, you haven't had any time to spend with any other young men."

"Mother, please, is it not enough for you to simply know that I am not in love with Prince Lagan?"

"Absolutely not!" Hermena's nostrils flared as she took another step towards her daughter. "I have spent too much of my time preparing you for an advantageous marriage. You will not waste all my efforts with your silly, girlish fancies!"

"It is my right to choose who I marry!"

"It has never been your right. You will choose who we choose for you!"

"Father, please help her see reason!"

But her father had had enough of bickering for one day. His whole life he wanted nothing more than peace and quiet and the contentment of his papyri. This drama was too much for him.

"I do not see why this needs to be decided right now. Both of you are too distraught to see reason. Let us have our dinner and talk about it in the morrow."

At the staircase, Psyche caught a glimpse of Claudia. She suddenly hoped that she could find a friend and confidante in the only other female in the house, but her sister's smugness stopped her.

"What a stupid girl you are," Claudia murmured.

"What do you mean?"

"You have everything, the gods have given you everything, and you waste it away. For a poor, dirty shepherd."

Psyche could not understand how Claudia could make her love for Erik sound so awful. Before she could respond, Claudia continued.

"Don't think that I don't know. That I didn't see you ogling him during the banquet. He's pretty enough, I suppose, if that's your type. But you'll be nothing but a poor shepherd's wife, with calluses from carding wool and butchering meat, back breaking work from what I hear. You'll become ugly and gnarled and you'll grow to hate him, and he you, because you'll be disgusting to look at. That's the life you'll choose over luxury, over being a princess? You are a bigger fool than I ever imagined. You'll be like mother. Hating your husband in the end. Hating your life and blaming your children."

Psyche took a deep breath, unshed tears of humiliation were stinging her eyes. How difficult it was to build dreams high until it reached the sun and beyond.

And how easy it was to crush them.

# Chapter 17

Eros felt filthy and degraded in every way. Fearing that his mother would never leave, he dropped a potion into her wine knowing that he needed her preoccupied for the evening so that he and Psyche could make their escape. If all worked well, the potion would keep her away for several days.

At first, the drink did not seem to have any effect on Aphrodite. Finally, he saw her nod off against a bullheaded creature she had been using as a chair. Eventually, she led the Minotaur to her bedchamber. Eros immediately peeled away from the intoxicated wood nymphs who had spent the night undulating before him. After a few pokes with his arrows, they were so engrossed in each other that they did not notice him go.

Just as he was leaving, a winged servant intercepted him with a message. Hermes would like to see him at his favorite tavern.

Eros looked at the moon hesitantly. He still had a few hours left before he was to meet Psyche.

Eros took himself to another corner of Olympus where Hermes was waiting for him in a popular tavern. The festive hall was a contrast to Eros's mood, but he entered anyway.

Eros saw Hermes smoking from a long, cylindrical tube near a group of young musicians, occasionally picking up his lyre and adding his own solo to the melodious entertainment. His voice was rich and deep, and the women sighed deeply at his soulful tenor.

Eros waited for the song to be done and had wine served to him in the meantime. A handful of deities were clustered in a corner murmuring grimly to each other. By a huge, cascading fountain with a sculpture of frolicking sea creatures, another group of demi-gods were laughing and petting a giant white tigress, sitting placidly on a giant cushion.

A serving girl with the tail of a serpent approached and offered Eros a tray of ripe fruit that he politely refused. He sat down and waited for Hermes.

When Hermes finally returned from the world of Muses, he spotted Eros and immediately bowed courteously to the other musicians before sauntering towards him.

Facing each other, Eros and Hermes made a striking contrast at the table. The maidens in the room began to argue which they preferred more.

The two seemed unaware of the affect they caused.

"Eros, I am glad you've come. I wanted to warn you that your mother had been looking for you these past few days."

"Your warning came a little bit too late. She was waiting for me at my palace before I arrived."

Hermes looked slightly uncomfortable beneath his friend's gaze. "Zeus's balls," he cursed under his breath.

Eros stared at him, realizing something. "She seemed to know a few things that I wasn't quite prepared for her to know."

Hermes was avoiding his eyes. "Is that so? I can't imagine how."

"Can you not?"

Eros's eyes were penetrating and Hermes could not meet his gaze. Instead, he cleared his throat noisily and took another swallow of the mysterious green ale in his hand.

"Have you tried this? It's a drink concocted by Sinatra herself. Absinthial, I think she calls it. I hope man never gets a hold of it. It is liquid evil, I tell you!"

"Fascinating. Were you drinking it when you told my mother all my secrets?"

"Oh, come now, don't place all of it on me. She has spies everywhere. She knew everything as it was."

Eros could barely contain his anger. "I see."

"It's the drink. You should blame Sinistra for inventing it. I will be honest with you Eros, you deserve to know. Your mother came upon me quite unexpectedly last night, right in my quarters. And you know how persuasive she is. That is why I asked you here tonight. I wanted to warn you."

"For the messenger god, your timing is quite awful."

Hermes looked genuinely distraught.

Eros leaned forward, his blue eyed glittering with rage. "How much did you tell her?"

"Nothing, except what she already knew. She noticed that you seemed to be taking much longer with Psyche than she thought

134

necessary. I told her jokingly that you couldn't be blamed being that the girl was supposed to be the most beautiful maiden on earth. She didn't like that comment too much."

"What did you tell her?"

"Nothing. Please, don't look at me like that. When I realized what she was up to, I clammed up. She wasn't interested in me, only in what I knew of you. That was clear enough after a while."

"After you made advances and she refused them."

"Not like that..."

"Of course like that."

Hermes set his drink down. "I clammed up because I'm your loyal friend. Your ingratitude astounds me sometimes."

"Ingrat—."

"Ah, don't lose your temper in a public place. All of Olympus will know. And you know how awful Sinistra gets when you break one of her crystal chalices. There will be Hades to pay."

"What did you tell her?" Eros's voice had taken a more vicious tone, but he still held it low.

"I told her that your loyalty was always towards her, and that she should trust you, and that she should not worry. I do not believe I said anything else."

"I should have known not to have trusted you."

"I protected you," Hermes protested.

"You didn't even warn me!"

"I tried, didn't I? How was I to know she'd reach you before my note did?"

"Your All-Seeing eye must not have been working very well tonight. Or perhaps the maidens you were flirting with earlier were more important than the well-being of an old friend?"

"Oh come now, your hit is needlessly hard, Eros. You are still here, aren't you? Your mortal girl is yet unharmed. Aphrodite must not have been too angry. Your head is still between your shoulders."

"For now!" Irritated with his friend, he got up to leave. "You disappoint me, Hermes. I do not think I can call you friend after this."

135

"If I were you, I would stay a while." Hermes was gazing passed him and Eros turned to see that Ares had just entered the tavern. "You would not wish to be followed."

"By the gods, everything is going wrong tonight!"

Hermes stared at Eros's haggard form and knew he had to make it up to his friend. He placed an assuring hand on Eros's shoulder and spoke loudly so that Ares could hear.

"You sound like you need another drink, lad. Sinistra! Another cup of wine for my friend here. He has had a rough evening. Seems like he's chasing after a girl who won't have him."

The serpentine server arrived, her beautiful, snakelike body encircling Hermes's waist seductively as she served Eros another cup of wine. "Not have him? Is she woman or fool?"

Hermes chuckled. "Both apparently."

"And for you, my lord?" She murmured into his ear.

"For me.... Ah, how you distract me so! I cannot think when you're near. Come back in three minutes and I'll give you my answer."

Eros looked away before he could see what the serpent's errant tail had started doing before she departed slowly.

"I never knew you were such a prude," Hermes noted with all too knowing eyes.

"It is not right to read minds among friends," Eros reminded him. He hated how he was always at a disadvantage.

"Ah, so you're my friend again! Believe me, I wasn't. It is written all over your face. I am not too drunk to sense when something is amiss."

"But you were yesterday when you revealed all of my secrets."

"Not all of them. And I have already apologized. I'd give you my soul if I had one."

When Eros said nothing, Hermes took another sip of his cup. He wanted to help but he also knew Eros would never tell him.

"She said 'yes', didn't she."

Eros stared at his uncle.

"No, I didn't read your mind, but it is all over your face. You're as transparent as this crystal chalice. She actually said 'yes.' She agreed to marry poor Erik the lowly sheepherder."

Eros remained silent and Hermes leaned back on his cushions. To Eros's irritation, he chuckled. "She is not a girl with very high standards, is she?"

When the younger man stood up, Hermes immediately shut his mouth and grasped the hand of the seething god.

"Oh, sit, sit, man. You are already making a scene with all your sulking. One might mistake you for the god of war instead of love. Not much hope you give humanity. Sit, sit."

Eros sat and immediately put his head in his hand. He had made such a tangle of everything. How could he protect Psyche from his mother? How could he protect her from Zeus? Marriage between a god and a mortal was forbidden. Copulation of any sort with mortals was frowned upon for the children from such unions were often monstrosities whose painful birth could kill their mothers. How could he risk that with Psyche? Zeus had his mortal women, but it was not for the likes of Eros to follow suit.

If Zeus found out about Psyche, he would finally have reason to confiscate Eros's arrows.

"Well, you are definitely in a bit of a rut," Hermes shifted in his seat sympathetically. "Marry her, and you risk the wrath of Zeus and your mother. Not marry her, and she will hate you forever. To me, it is a simple choice, but then, I am not in love."

"Why do you think love complicates things?"

"Because those who feel it seem to lose their understanding of right and wrong!" Hermes did not miss the irony of the moment, but he was the only one smiling.

"You don't think love might help us see things more clearly?"

"No," he responded without the slightest hesitation and set his drink down. "I think love clouds our judgment. I think it is a weapon that can be used against us."

Eros looked back at his friend and suddenly knew why Hermes feared him. Eros had never bothered to shoot Hermes with his arrows because he always liked his friend.

That could change. And Hermes knew this.

"You don't think love itself has any value?"

Hermes leaned back and looked at him wryly. "I don't," he admitted. "But I am not you. You should determine the value of love. You are a god who wields its power."

Eros thought about Psyche, about the bracelet she made for him, remembering her eyes when she gave it to him. Her capacity ran deep. Deeper than most mortals. She was unafraid. And with her, perhaps, he could finally understand love. Not just infatuation, not just lust, words which were always confused with love, which Hermes seemed to use interchangeably, but Love in its full potential. Love, in its ultimate and purest form. Whatever it looked like, Eros needed to know. And only Psyche could show him.

"Hush! Control your thoughts, Ares is on his way!"

Eros immediately blanked his mind as a heavy hand landed on his shoulder. Eros looked up to see the towering god of war looming above him.

"Young Eros. I didn't think I'd see you here."

Ares was more than a formidable man. He was monstrous and for the millionth time, Eros wondered what his mother saw in such a bear of man with no remnant of wit, intellect, or charm.

Eros managed a greeting. "Lord Ares, how are you this evening?"

"Very good. Very good. How is that beautiful mother of yours? I have not seen her in almost two nights. Is your father on holiday again and keeping her locked up?"

It was a low blow, but then Ares always went for the low blows. Hermes whistled, and called for another cup of Absynthia.

"If you mean Hephaestus, he is working like always. As for mother, why, she is as wonderful as ever," Eros responded. "Last I saw, she was falling asleep in the arms of a Minotaur, perhaps someone she considers a cleverer, more charming bedmate than what she's had lately."

Ares made a sound that was almost a snarl. Hermes coughed and hid his laughter in another sip of drink.

"Watch yourself, little boy. I have crushed men ten times your size with my bare hands."

Hermes held up his hand. "Let us not quarrel tonight, friend Ares. I hear the battle is raging in Troy. You must be exhausted from all the bloodshed."

Ares waved his hand. "I never tire of bloodshed. Hear that, Eros. But the Greeks are resting up for easy pickings in the light. Troy continues to burn." The disappointment was thick in his voice.

"Ah, so you are passing the time here at Mt. Olympus."

"Indeed." Ares took another sip of his ale and stared at Eros. "I also have other matters to attend to. I'm to keep an eye on this one. His mummy doesn't want him straying too far from the nest."

"Most interesting," Hermes did not look very interested at all, but Eros recognized the signal not to appear too alarmed.

"It is good of you, Ares, to keep my mother entertained while I am away," Eros placed his hand heavily on his shoulder. Ares glared at the hand. Eros tried not to show his intimidation as he plowed on. "It is good to know that there are still gods who are not too proud or boastful to keep the womenfolk happy during times of duress. I see Athena is not here tonight. She must be caught up in some petty war stratagem or other."

Hermes smiled and looked at his friend knowingly. "Now that is a woman who needs to learn to relax and have some fun."

Ares frowned. "Athena is not in Olympus? Is she helping the Greeks with the fire perhaps?"

"Who knows," Eros shrugged, lifting his wine to Sinistra, who winked suggestively. "Or cares. It is much more pleasant here without her."

"Indeed," Hermes added. "Athena is always trying to make the rest of us look bad. Working day and night like she does non-stop. I don't know what she is trying to prove."

Eros nodded. "She doesn't seem to know that Zeus will always favor gods over goddesses. It doesn't matter how dedicated she is, or hard working."

"She could live in Troy and Zeus would never notice," Hermes added.

"If he did, we might truly be in trouble."

Hermes lifted his hands to signal. "Sinistra, my dear, some Absynthia for our good friend Ares here. He needs a break from that

139

wretched war. Look how tired he seems! Won't some lady come and help our poor hero with a well-deserved respite?"

Several began to volunteer, but Ares stood before Sinistra could arrive, his brow troubled.

Athena was Ares's rival. Relaxing while there was a war going on would not bode well in Zeus's eyes. The reminder was much needed. He would be damned if he would be outshone by a woman!

"No drink. I must go now."

Eros looked up with disappointment. "But, I thought you were to keep an eye on me. What will my mother say?"

"I have more important things to do than follow orders from womenfolk."

"Well said!" Hermes exclaimed. "Make sure you tell that to Athena next time she tries to tell you what to do."

"I trust Hermes will keep you in check, little dove boy. He should know that lying to Aphrodite or any god is a slap in the face of Zeus."

"Hermes will keep me company in this happy little tavern all night, Ares. We are sorry you cannot join us."

He grunted and stalked off, snarling at a griffin that accidentally crossed his path. The usually fierce creature whimpered and scuttled away.

As soon as the unwanted company left, Eros stood up.

Hermes frowned. "You're leaving, too? So soon?"

The look on the young god's face made Hermes's heart turn cold. "You plan to marry the girl?"

When Eros did not answer, Hermes cried out, "Are you daft? You will lose everything!"

"Everything is worth nothing without her."

Hermes watched, jaw still open, as Eros disappeared. He sat back down and told himself he should keep away. He told himself that Eros's troubles were not his and that the Fates should have to decide his destiny. But in another instant, he was putting his chalice down.

"Where are you off to in such a rush?" Sinistra purred, suddenly blocking his path with her snake tail.

"I am off to save a friend from perhaps the biggest mistake of his life."

"That is quite noble of you."

"Hah, hardly noble. Just trying to save myself." With a devilish smile, he winked at the vermillion creature and hurried on his way.

# Chapter 18

Psyche sat picking at her food miserably, trying to ignore the stabbing glares from her mother's direction.

Her father touched her hand from across the table.

"My dear, perhaps it would be easier if you simply tell us who this other fellow is. Perhaps we are all getting into a fuss for nothing."

When she remained silent, he sighed and leaned back on the chair. "Remember our talk that one day, when we were hunting. You know what I said to you then? That I would never give you away to the highest bidder. You must trust me, my dear, no matter what your mother might insist. Tell the parents who love you so very much who they can expect for their son in law."

The request sounded so reasonable, and Psyche was on the verge of telling her father everything. Then she caught her mother's glance, a faint narrowing of her eyes as she gazed upon her husband. Psyche changed her mind.

But she had to give them an answer, and as much as it hurt her to lie to her father, she also couldn't run the risk of her mother doing something to stop her from meeting Erik that night.

"It... it is ... nobody. I am not in love with anybody. You were right, Mother, when you said that I only said it in a panic, to get Prince Lagan to give me some more time. I... I don't have any other man in mind."

Her father seemed satisfied with this answer, and although her mother eyed her suspiciously, she said nothing.

"Well, my dear, that sounds quite understandable to me." Her father patted her gently on her hand. "I admit, it must have been a bit of a shock. You have only just been returned to us and now you may have to leave again to get married. Perhaps Prince Lagan will understand your desire to stay with us a bit longer before the nuptials. In the morrow, we'll have a talk, all of us including the prince, and clear everything up."

Psyche squeezed his hand back. She looked at his sweet face lovingly, wondering if she would ever see it again. She hated lying to him, yet, she could see no other way. The dinner continued in silence, her mother too angry to speak to anyone and only Psyche's father tried to make conversation, which was quite a daunting task for a man who did not often talk. Psyche helped as much as she could, making sure she remembered every little detail of him.

Before bed, Psyche gathered enough things for a few days of travel and tucked it under her pillow. She also took the few coins she had saved up all her life. She put on a short tunic under her nightgown before she went to bed.

She lay in bed waiting for the rest of the house to fall asleep.

Waiting was the hardest part. She closed her eyes and relived the entire afternoon again. She thought of the way the sun's rays danced upon Erik's beautiful face. The way his smile made her breath catch in her throat. Just the memory of it was causing her to do it again.

Then she remembered his kisses. And his hands. Oh, those hands! She blushed when she thought of them. The smell and the taste of him. He was perfect. She couldn't believe he was hers. She did not think a lifetime with him would be enough to satisfy her need of him. She couldn't wait to hear his voice again. To hear his heart thudding so powerfully beneath her ear. To get to know him more and more deeply. To talk to him endlessly into the night and penetrate the mysterious wall he always seemed to have around him. He was the most fascinating man she had ever met.

And he was hers.

She thought she would die of ecstasy.

When she saw a figure open her door, Psyche willed herself to be as still as possible and continued her deep breathing. Finally, the figure moved away.

Psyche waited for another hour. But she was content making plans. They would elope, find a priest of the temple of Hera, goddess of marriage, and pay him to perform the marriage rites. Then, they would travel on Erik's donkey to Pella, which was about two day's journey away. Then they would go on to Erik's home town and meet his family. She hoped they would be accepting of her. Indeed, without her parent's blessings, she would come with no dowry, nothing to offer. But she was sure Erik would help convince them.

And perhaps in time, they would accept that she had other things to offer.

When the house was completely still, Psyche slowly pulled her sack out of the pillow and carried her boots in her hands. The wood creaked under her feet, but she was careful about where she placed her foot on the floorboards. Just as she reached her bedroom window, she heard a voice behind her.

"Where do you think you're going?"

Psyche jumped and looked in terror at the source. Her mother stood at the doorway.

Knowing there was no escape in lying, she raised her head slightly and looked straight at her mother.

"I am leaving."

"Stupid girl!" She hissed. "Go back to bed this instant!"

"No, mother."

"You will go back now or I will wake up your father and have him lock you in here."

"Then bid him!"

Without another word, Psyche jumped out the window. She grabbed onto a branch that she had always used to sneak out of her house and swung safely to the ground. Behind her, she could hear her mother screeching for her husband. She paused only to pull her boots on then raced across the field.

She ran as fast as she could, knowing that her father would reach her soon. But that didn't stop her. She crossed the valley and climbed a hill before thrashing into the forest. She was surprised she had made it this far, but she also knew that the closer she got to Erik, the harder it would be for her father to drag her kicking and screaming back to the house.

While walking through familiar trails, she heard her father behind her on horseback. There was no escaping him on foot. Still, she scurried behind a rock and waited for him to pass. After the horse thundered by, she moved to run, then stopped herself. Ahead of her was a beautiful mulberry tree, its moss covered trunk soft and inviting. She walked slowly towards the tree and sighed, knowing he would find her eventually. She touched the fruit sadly. She hoped she could make him understand.

144

It didn't take her father long to realize he had lost her trail and turn back. She could see him approaching the tree.

He looked tired, out of breath and extremely worried. Psyche was sorry she caused so much trouble. But it could not be helped.

"Psyche?"

"You told me that you would never sell me to the highest bidder."

He sighed with relief, seeing her safe and whole. "It is dangerous to run off in the night like that. There are wild cats and wolves out here. Weren't you the one who sang of Pyramus and Thisbe? And here you are under a mulberry tree, the scene of tragedy."

"I had no other choice."

"Of course, you did."

"Mother controls you, father! When she is in the room, it is like you become a different person."

He stared at her, looking suddenly haggard. "I'm... sorry. I know it must seem that way, but she understands these things better than I."

"Meaning that she is a woman so she must understand her daughters better than you. I am not just a woman, father. I am a free thinking human being just like you!"

"I know that. Of course I know that, and you more than anyone."

"Then why do you allow her to cart me off like chattel? Sell me to a prince with fat pockets so she could raise herself to a higher level."

"Not just herself, all of us. You as well. It is not selfish to want what is best for everyone in the end."

"Except me."

"How do you know this?"

"Because I don't love the prince."

"Love. Is love enough anymore?"

"You used to say it was."

"My darling, if you only knew what that woman gave up for me."

"For love!"

145

"For... nothing. I am nothing. Just a poor farmer with his head always in the clouds."

"For a man who worships her. And loves her so much, he lets her get away with anything, include making his youngest daughter so very unhappy."

"My daughter, I will never make you do anything you don't want to. You think I cannot stand up to my own wife. What little you think of me! I love your mother, that is true. Very much. But I also love you and your sisters. And that has to count for something. I always thought you liked Prince Lagan."

"I do like him, but I do not love him. And I do not wish to marry him."

"Then you do not have to. I will speak to your mother. But there is no need for you to run about in the night like this alone. The woods are far too dangerous. And you are far too precious. We have time. Like I said, you need not rush anything. Tomorrow—"

"No. Father, I can't. I must go. He is waiting for me."

"Daughter… You said there was no one else."

Her expression gave him the answer.

"Then who is it? What man would you go to such great lengths to be with?"

Psyche looked at her father and made a decision.

Eros was on the hill minutes before the second hour. He was only mildly disappointed that she had not arrived yet. It gave him a bit more time to plan.

He had made the decision to try to live the remainder of Psyche's life as a human. He would get himself to age in the same manner she aged, and they could spend what time they had together in married bliss.

If they had children... well, he would worry about that when the time came.

Then, there was the fear of what Eros would do when her mortal heart stopped beating. Perhaps he could become one of Death's disciples and turn his back on the living forever.

But that was yet, another decision he could make later.

146

For now, it was enough just to be with her. There was a place in Cyprus they could hide in. He had friends who owed him favors. Perhaps he could put her to sleep briefly and they could be there before the sun was up. It would save them both a dangerous and tiring journey by foot. He could tell her she had fallen ill, which was why she did not remember most of the journey.

Lies.

There would never be an end to them. And yet, that was the price he would have to pay. There was no other way, unless.... No, he couldn't tell her. It was too dangerous. But, perhaps in time he could explain to her, little by little, slowly as not to shock her. And as not to alarm the gods.

When Eros heard a noise behind him, he turned with a ready smile. So like his Psyche to come exactly on the hour.

"My love—"

The words died on his lips and he cursed.

"Eros, I cannot allow you to do this."

Hermes stood before him, his face a thundercloud, devoid of all humor. Eros did not respond, but straightened his back to a position more fitting for a god than a sheepherder.

"Hermes, you are not needed here."

"Have you gone mad? You know this is against Zeus's rules."

"Zeus is not my only commander. My heart bids me to do this."

"Your heart! Such a callous, silly little thing!" Rage fired in Hermes's eyes. "If you were going to take such a grave risk, could you not have thought of a better plan? Cyprus? Really? To lie for the rest of her life? Eros, you are not a boy anymore! You have to make smarter decisions than this."

"This does not concern you!"

"You are breaking a thousand laws by being here!"

"And since when were you protector of all laws. You, the god of lies and trickery!"

Eros's anger caused his wings to sprout. The golden glow surrounding him was brighter than the full moon in the crisp night.

147

Hermes followed, allowing his full godly form to brighten the once dark and quiet clearing.

Shadowy creatures raced away in fright.

"I am here in the name of Zeus. To save you from yourself. How could you be so foolish as to not see this?"

"Leave now." Eros glared at his uncle.

"I am not leaving without you." With that, Hermes reached for Eros, who swung away and pushed him with a force that sent him staggering to a nearby tree.

Shocked by the attack, Hermes shook the dizziness in his head.

"You ridiculous child!" Enraged, Hermes sent a beam of light straight at Eros that pinned him instantly to the thick willow, its leaves spreading like curtains at the force. Suddenly the beam stopped as Hermes looked distractedly at a puddle at his feet. Their activities were causing a stir. The gods were looking towards them. Including Ares.

Free from the light beam, Eros grabbed a huge boulder and flung it at the distracted god.

The force pushed Hermes over the edge of the cliff, falling to the ground.

Eros knew he needed to find Psyche quickly. To protect her. To take her away with him and escape Olympus forever. Before he could go, the leaves of the willow wrapped themselves around him. He cursed as Hermes reappeared above the cliff.

"Do you not understand?" Hermes shouted. "Ares is on his way. You must make haste now, back to the tavern. It is the only way to save yourself."

Eros struggled and managed to get one of his arrows to slice the branches that held him. "I am not afraid of that brute!"

Eros disappeared into the woods and Hermes flew towards the branches after him.

An arrow flew into the trees passed him. At first, Hermes thought Eros had aimed and missed, only to see that he had intentionally struck a cougar hiding in the branches. Upon seeing Hermes, the animal leapt on top of the god and tried to wrestle him. Hermes pushed the animal away and tried to shoot Eros again with a beam of light, but missed the speeding god. The beam scattered in a burst of sparkles that turned the green foliage red.

"Bold words until you see what Ares does to you before he presents your head to your mother. She will then reward him generously after feeding you to his horses!"

There was only silence as Hermes peered into the darkness. Eros was disguised again, but he saw the shepherd and flew at him.

"Think, man! It will be the end of both you and Psyche. Aphrodite will not rest until that girl is finished. And she will make sure she suffers first! Psyche will suffer more because of you!"

"Aphrodite would have to get through me first!"

Hermes caught up at last and grabbed the younger god's neck with a deathly hold.

"Stupid boy! She does not have to get through you, Ares will." Hermes was shocked when Eros flipped him around and threw him at another tree which fell back instantly at the force. Before his uncle could recuperate, Eros charged full force towards him and pushed him to the ground.

Hermes struggled, surprised by Eros's strength. But the younger god was weakening. Suddenly, an arrow was pointed at Hermes's throat.

The messenger god froze.

"I could make you fall in love with her, too. Then you would be forced to protect her."

"You're completely mad."

"Then leave us be."

"To do what?"

"We will run."

Eros panted as his uncle continued to struggle beneath his hold.

"To where?" Hermes choked. "For how long? If it's not Ares who will catch up with you, it will be Zeus himself."

Hermes looked at the set jaw and determined face. He broke the rules of friendship and read Eros's mind.

Hermes's fears were confirmed. He saw fury and desperation. He also saw fear. Eros knew he was committing suicide by marrying Psyche. And he was doing it all so he could understand something. Even if it was for one night. *One night?*

Had Hermes read that right? He would give everything up for one night with her?

Eros was thinking like a mortal. No, he was thinking like an impulsive, savage animal. All he cared about was instant gratification.

Hermes was furious.

Past his nephew's head, Hermes saw the light of Ares descending quickly upon them.

"Then you leave me no choice."

Before Eros could get wind of his intentions, Hermes grabbed him by his neck and kicked his heels, making him fly straight up, taking his stubborn nephew with him, a flash of lightning streaking straight across the sky to the other side of the world.

The only sign that the gods were once there was a small white feather that drifted slowly down to the center of the clearing.

# Chapter 19

When Psyche and her father arrived, they were almost an hour late, but she was certain Erik would still be waiting. She called out to him and began searching around the perimeter, instructing her father to stay in case he arrived.

Her father had been disappointed by the name she had given for her future husband, but he was more disappointed that Erik had not come to him first. Even if he disapproved, even if he told him, "no," it was what men of courage did.

"Erik is a man of courage," Psyche insisted. "He just did not want to disobey you or to put you in a position where you have to oppose your wife."

"That is a choice for me to make, not him."

He did, however, agree that he needed to speak to Erik himself and clear up any misunderstandings they might have of each other. Only then, would he give his blessing.

The idea that her father may give his blessing at all made Psyche happy. When Erik was nowhere to be found, she settled next to her father beneath the willow tree.

"Perhaps he got held back for a bit, as I did."

"Perhaps," her father responded impassively.

The look he gave her made Psyche lift her chin a little higher. "He will come."

Her father looked away into the moonlight. He knew when it was pointless to argue. After a while, he pulled out his short sword and began sharpening it. It was not sinister, he simply needed to keep himself busy for he had a feeling it would be a very long night.

When dawn came, Psyche's father stood up. His daughter was staring out at the sunrise, but he knew she was not seeing anything. He took a deep breath. A part of him was relieved that the boy never showed up. But he was also not looking forward to dragging his daughter away from the hilltop.

Ares watched from a distance. He had arrived shortly after Psyche and her father and he was surprised that no one else was there.

Someone had rung the warning bells for Eros, and he suspected he knew who it was.

Nevertheless, the little scene with the older man and his stubborn daughter entertained him. The man was nothing but patience and Ares was surprised he didn't give the silly girl the thrashing she deserved. Ares would have enjoyed the show.

By Zeus, she was a sight to behold in the flesh! With that short tunic, and wild multi-colored hair. She had a bold air about her that was rare in a mortal woman. Her spirit begged to be broken. Now she was fighting her father with wild abandon, insisting that they needed to form a search party. That "Erik" must be dying somewhere.

Her passion aroused Ares. If Aphrodite weren't in the picture, he would have taken the mortal for himself. But Aphrodite was not fond of sharing. Even if he explained to her the circumstance. That he would only keep her until he tired of her, or until he accidentally killed her in his excitement. It was not uncommon for a god to do such a thing to a mortal lover. It was one of the reasons it was forbidden. And Ares was an especially ardent partner. He would be serving Aphrodite a justice, completing the punishment her son clearly did not have the prowess to give. If this Psyche mortal wanted to be beneath a real man, he was certain he could satisfy her in ways Eros never could.

Still, it was not meant to be. He did not know which of the pathetic mortals would be her new choice, but this was no longer any of his affair. He would report back to his goddess, and no doubt, she would be too displeased to pay him any attention. This was a most disappointing turn of events. He truly was looking forward to seeing the beating that insolent young son of hers was going to receive.

It was time Eros was raised with a much firmer hand.

When Hermes finally released Eros, they were not too far away from Atlas bearing the burden of the sky upon his shoulder. They had not flown for long, but Hermes was known as the fastest god in Olympus for a reason.

Once Hermes released his young nephew, Eros struck him.

Hermes saw stars for a few moments, but was impressed by the young god's ferocity. He could never get used to such viciousness from the god of love.

Before Hermes could respond, Eros let out an agonized cry that shook Hermes to the core. Hermes immediately sobered.

"Hush! All of Olympus will hear!"

"Why?" Eros demanded not lowering his voice. "Why did you stop me? It was not your decision to make!"

"Eros, you are not thinking straight. If you were, you would have made the right decision. But, that woman put a spell on you!"

"I do not care. I do not care! You know nothing of me or of love!"

The comment did have an affect on Hermes. The darkness of his eyes looked terrifying on a face usually so light with humor. "I know more than you can ever realize. I know enough to know it can destroy without a thought, that it can bring down the strongest, most noble of men. It can start wars and cause death and destruction of the likes this world has never seen before. And it can bring a god of otherwise sound mind to the brink of insanity!"

"You know only the bad. You know only its destructive powers. You know nothing of its joy. Nothing of its hope…" Without another word, Eros's wings burst from his back and he flew as fast as he could back towards the hilltop where he hoped Psyche still waited.

Hermes stood and watched, shaking his head. He had done his best. If the boy wanted to race towards his own demise, there was nothing more he could do. He could only hope that the journey would knock some sense into him.

By the time Eros arrived on the hilltop, exhausted, the sun was low in the sky. Psyche was nowhere. He knew she would have felt broken, betrayed, and it would be difficult to explain to her. He needed only to go to her home and plead with her family. He needed only to…

He needed only to lie some more.

The flight had quelled some of his madness. The more he thought about it, the more foolish his plan seemed to be. If he were caught and punished, what would become of Psyche? He knew what he was risking for being with her, but she had no idea what she was walking into or who it was she was marrying or who it was she was risking her unborn children for. What right did he have to put her in such danger without her complete knowledge?

The truth was one he feared more than anything else. More than his mother's wrath. More than Zeus.

He was afraid that she wouldn't love him if she knew. But the truth was, she did not really love him at all. She loved Erik, an invented shepherd with an invented life. How was that love?

He was no different from his philandering grandfather. Psyche deserved better. She deserved the truth. But how could he tell her without bringing on the wrath of Olympus?

One thing was for certain, it was not something he could plan and execute tonight. Psyche deserved love, in its purest most untainted form. And he could not provide that for her.

Not yet.

It was with a heavy heart that Eros looked about him one last time at the spot that had offered so much hope for him just a few hours ago. She had been here, he was certain of it, she had waited for him. He could still smell her scent by the willow.

Eros touched the bracelet on his wrist, remembering her eyes the instant she gave it to him. The love in them. But it was not love for him. It was for Erik, the lucky bastard. Erik, who he must turn his back on forever. The shield that a god was hiding behind, coward that he was.

He could only hope that the woman who gave him this bracelet could learn to love him again. Not Erik, but Eros. And not even Eros. Not the one she read of. A never-do-well, cullion, miscreant, wastrel. All words he deserved at one point or another. But a new Eros. A new god of love. One worthy of her.

A god, he mused, struggling to be worthy of a mortal woman. But he no longer felt like this was such a revolutionary concept. God, demi-god, mortal, one ought to be judged beyond such labels. One ought to be judged by ones true worth, by ones immortal soul.

Eros turned his back from the clearing, from the innocence of his mortal form, and the future that could never be.

Perhaps it was foolish for him to believe that he could ever truly defy the gods. Perhaps he should have known that the Fates would never have allowed him true happiness.

But Psyche needed to be kept safe. Somehow. The more time he spent with her, the more risk he was putting her in. Perhaps one day she will come to know how much this moment had cost him, and how much he hated doing it. But for now, there were more important things to take care of than a broken heart.

Eros shot up into the air, knowing that he didn't have a moment to lose.

# Chapter 20

Psyche initially worried that Erik had been hurt or wounded, mauled by a cougar or pinned beneath a boulder screaming for help. Eventually, news from Lucius arrived that Erik had been seen at the alehouse not too long ago that evening. Erik told everyone that he had to leave and most likely would never return. He asked that Lucius give Psyche and her family his regards.

While dining with the family, Lucius surreptitiously gave Psyche a scrap of papyri under the table. "He told me to give you this and made me promise on the heart of Hermes that I would not read it or let anyone know."

With trembling fingers, Psyche opened the note. Could it be more instructions about how to meet? Had he seen her father with her and felt betrayed?

Something fell from the scrap. With trembling fingers, she picked up the bracelet she had given Erik yesterday afternoon off the floor. The tears began to form and she could hardly read the scrawl on the parchment. It contained only two lines. The lines were crooked, she knew it must have been difficult for him to write. As a teacher, she couldn't help feeling a bit proud of him.

"P and T shall live. Be happy."

*P and T.* Psyche could barely process the letters. She merely clutched the bracelet and let the tears fall.

"Psyche, are you unwell?"

Her father's voice could barely penetrate her mind. A mind that still couldn't believe Erik was truly gone. That he had truly left. With nothing but this and lines she didn't even understand.

"I am unwell, father. I think I need to lie down."

"Of course."

Psyche stumbled away.

P and T shall live?

Then, she understood. Pyramus and Thisbe. An alternate ending. Erik and Psyche were like a retelling of the old story, only both lived. They can only survive by being apart, obeying the rules, and letting their families dictate their lives. He was telling her to accept this. To be happy.

Psyche fell upon her bed and allowed herself to weep. She raged against the covers, wondering how he could do this to her, how he could leave her without even saying good-bye.

She vaguely remembered someone knocking on her door, her mother leaving her food by her bed, all of which remained untouched.

Erik had left her. At first, she could not accept it. As the days went by, she found herself looking out of her window expecting him to arrive on his donkey with apologetic eyes, telling her that he had gotten cold feet but now realized that he could not live without her. She clung to the bracelet she made, the grass had dried but was still strong, designed to last. She thought of how she would react when he did come. She would be cold and distant to him at first, make him understand how cruelly he had acted, but in the end, she would melt into his embrace and beg him never to leave her like that again.

But he never came.

He sent no other word. He had no excuse not to do this. He had learned his letters. He could have sent her another note to tell her that he had arrived safely back to his village.

But nothing.

Psyche did not leave her house, she moved without direction, ate without taste. Her mother continued to give her orders all of which she did, wanting to keep her hands busy, to keep her mind occupied, to stop herself from waiting by the window and wasting away. But at night, when all was still and quiet and all she had were her thoughts, she could only think of her future, a stretch of bland possibilities that carried no thrill and no hope. Psyche allowed the tears to fall. They were calmer now, less intense than that first night, but sadder somehow. What was she going to do? How was she going to survive? Everything was paler, more colorless. She did not think she could ever smile again.

Prince Lagan, having heard of her escapade in the middle of the night to see another man, was so deeply offended that he did not wish to see her ever again. As unhappy as her mother was by this, Psyche was surprised that she did not press the matter. Perhaps there was something in her daughter's eyes that finally stayed Hermena's tongue. Still, other admirers continued to wait for her, and her mother invited them in, but Psyche never came out of her room to receive any of them.

She could hear her mother and father arguing. She was surprised, for she had never heard her father raise his voice to her mother, but there it was.

"She needs time," he told her. "You cannot rush things like this. She will be back to herself soon."

But she wasn't. Not before the rumors started.

They began harmlessly enough. The villagers believed that Psyche had taken ill from a physically debilitating disease. One that might spread. The suitors were coming less and less. Psyche was relieved, her mother worried. Hermena went into town and overheard the conversations.

"It is not natural for so much beauty in a single woman," the blacksmith's wife insisted. "She must have done something to displease the gods."

"I always knew that family would lead us to no good," added the tailor.

"All those men were falling all over themselves over that girl. It was like she had put a spell on them," said a third.

When the group of women saw Hermena approach them, they immediately turned away and pretended to be busy. Hermena saw Lucius and asked him brightly how his horses were doing. Lucius responded that he had lost two fowls recently and had been cleaning the stalls hoping to rid of whatever plague might have infected them. He promised to dine with the Halsteds when he resolved the issue. He asked about Psyche and Hermena watched the telltale blush on the young man's face. He had not lost interest in her daughter and at this point, the horse-trader was Hermena's only hope of making a decent family connection.

But the plague did not resolve and Lucius continued to stay away. In fact, it seemed to have affected all the village chattel. Livestock were falling without any reason. Cows, sheep, horses, swine, no animal was immune. At first, they seemed to target certain homes, homes with bachelors, men who had recently visited the house on Seventh Hill.

Then the floods began. Rain that began normally, given the time of year, ceased to stop. The rivers swelled unnaturally, flooding whole fields, then homes, washing away lives and livelihoods in a matter of days.

When the home of Claudius was completely covered in water, the villagers recalled an argument he'd had with Lucius a few weeks before, where he had said offensive things about the gods. Some were saying he had brought the wrath of Olympus upon himself. Lucius visited his old friend who he hadn't spoken to since that morning when they exchanged fists at the village square. He was a shadow of the man he remembered, his once proud shoulders slumped, and his hair was still wet having barely escaped death when the water poured into his home.

When Claudius saw the man at the door, he reached out his hand. "Lucius, friend, you must help me."

Lucius took the hand. "You may stay with me at my home for as long as you need."

The gratitude in the other man's eyes moved Lucius.

"Thank you," Claudius gasped. "You are a good man. I was a fool to have said what I said to you."

"It is already forgotten."

"But it shouldn't be! Everyone must be warned."

"What do you mean?"

"I had a dream. Or a vision. I do not know what it was. A being not of this world visited me. It said that I had to be punished. That I had offended the gods. I said I didn't mean to. That the witch, Psyche, had put me up to it."

"Psyche? A witch?"

"Of course! She clouds men's judgment. She makes them say horrible things. Blasphemous things!"

"Claudius, if I recall, you had said those words yourself. You had told me I would rather kiss the arse of Zeus than—."

"I know what I said! You needn't remind me. But that demoness, that temptress on Seventh Hill, she had me obsessed. She fed us blasphemy after blasphemy and turned me against the gods."

"Psyche has never been against the gods. She merely questions their methods sometimes and their reasoning."

"Sacrilege! You were right this whole time, Lucius. No one should question the gods. They are to be feared. They are to be obeyed. She is trouble for this village. She brought this whole thing upon us!"

Lucius put a hand on his friend's shoulder. "You are distraught. You have lost a great deal this day. Get some rest. Get some food in your stomach. We shall discuss this tomorrow."

But word only continued to spread. Claudius's dream was retold. It was Hermes who had visited him, enraged by his lack of piety. It was Aphrodite, others insisted, envious of Psyche's attention. Whoever it was, the village was in an uproar.

Psyche, the villagers proclaimed, had offended the gods and they put a curse on her and the village.

Lucius watched with growing uneasiness at the mob that was forming. He tried to reason with them, to explain that there must be some other explanation, but the evidence seemed to point toward Psyche. She had fallen ill and the problems of the village seemed to start soon after. Lucius suggested that the villagers make sacrifices to the temple of Aphrodite and pray for forgiveness. Flowers and gifts overwhelmed the small temple. Still, the rains would not stop.

Lucius stared at the marble statue of Aphrodite willing it to tell him what to do. His heart was reluctant to believe that Psyche was responsible for all this trouble, but the villagers wanted blood.

"I know you love her."

Lucius turned to see Claudius behind him.

"I do not," but he knew he wasn't convincing.

"If she is innocent, let her prove her innocence. Let her come and meet the Oracle of Aphrodite. Let him see the truth."

Lucius hesitated. If she were the cause of the rains, it would be a dark moment for Lucius. He had known Psyche almost all her life. She was one of his dearest friends before she became more to him. She never seemed to show him any special interest, but he was hoping this would change with time. Still, the gods were his leaders and they commanded his fate as well as the entire village.

Perhaps Psyche was clouding his judgment. What was one woman to an entire village of good people? If the gods did not favor her, then she was not the one for him. Lucius raised his head and turned to look at his friend.

"Let us go."

# Chapter 21

The knock of the door was loud and demanding, snapping Psyche out of her sad memories and causing Claudia to drop her weaving.

When Psyche opened it, she saw Lucius and three other men that Psyche recognized vaguely as past suitors. She did not remember their names, but she greeted them politely.

Lucius seemed surprised to see her. After all the rumors, he expected half her face to be eaten by some terrible plague. Instead, she looked as beautiful as ever, if a little pale. And upon close inspection, her cheeks did look more sunken, but in no way unattractive.

Despite Lucius's intent to be assertive with her and her family, he could not help bowing respectfully towards her. Psyche managed a weak smile that never reached her eyes. She allowed the men in. They did not accept her offer to sit. She continued to stand by the fireplace with them, starting to sense a tension.

"What brings you here today, Master Lucius?"

"I'm afraid I bear some bad news. There is talk at the village that the rains may have something to do with... you, Psyche."

"Me?"

Her father stood next to her and put a protective hand on her shoulder. "What is the meaning of this, Lucius? How could an innocent young woman cause such a thing?"

"If she's so innocent, then why hasn't she been down in the village for almost a full moon now?" Demanded the man to Lucius's right. He was burly and had long black curls twisting from his sideburns. "The instant she started to stay away was when the trouble started."

"Come now. A coincidence. Psyche is suffering from an ailment of the heart. Nothing more."

"Then why has the rain not stopped?" Demanded the other one just as burly with a more sour expression.

"I do not know. I am not Zeus."

The man took a step towards her father. "Watch it, little man. Your tone is offensive."

Psyche stood up, the fire springing back into her eyes. "How dare you enter our home and threaten a good, pious man like my father. Who are you and what do you want here? Lucius, you are a trusted friend and we allowed you into our hearth. Yet, you bring two walking cudgels with you. For shame!"

Lucius looked contrite. "I assure you, no one intends to do harm to anyone. I have brought them here to portray the growing unrest that the village is starting to feel. You are lucky that the mobs in the village have stayed away. There have been rumors that the shepherd may have..." Lucius turned a shade of pink that almost matched Claudia's rose-colored dress, and he cleared his throat delicately.

"Erik?" Her father clarified. "The shepherd, Erik, what does he have to do with anything?"

"We think he may have something to do with the curse this village is under."

"The village is not cursed," her father insisted.

"Well, there are others who would disagree. Erik spent some time here and—"

"There is not a bachelor alive in this village that did not spend time here."

"Yes, I know that, but his disappearance has worried some. And it seems to match your daughter's rumored illness."

"Lucius," Psyche stepped forward. "You can see for yourself. I am not ill. I am sorry for what the village is going through, but it has nothing to do with me."

Lucius looked and the other men leered. Psyche was indeed the peak of youth and health. He had missed looking at her. He had missed the pleasure it always brought him. He shook himself.

"There is only one way to know for sure," a man in a dark hood to the right of Lucius finally spoke. "We want you and your daughter to consult an Oracle in the temple of Aphrodite."

"An Oracle?"

"You must bring a sheep. A female as a sacrifice."

Before anyone could protest, Lucius added reassuringly, "It is standard practice. If you do not have one, I believe I could spare you one. If she has nothing to do with the terrible weather we're having, then it will be cleared up immediately. The Oracle will tell us."

"And if she does?"

No one in the room wanted to answer her father.

Psyche lifted her chin. "If I am the cause of so much grief, then I will gladly do what must be done to help the village. Until this is proven, however, I believe your men have no other business here. Unless, Lucius, you and your thugs wish to punish me right now without any proof of wrongdoing."

The gasp that came from her mother who had been silent up until now seemed to break the tension.

"Of course not," Lucius bowed, his face agitated. "We are a civilized people, Psyche. Good day, Master Halsted."

The temple of Aphrodite was crowded when Psyche and her father arrived. She was surprised by the open hostility some of the villagers were showing her. Psyche began to have her own doubts. The villagers seemed truly convinced that she was the cause of the floods and the disease. An apple core only barely missed her head and she gripped her father's hand and hurried inside the temple. Suddenly, she remembered the night when the men fell to their knees before her. She had been worried then, what the gods would think of such blatant adoration for a mere mortal, but her mother had insisted that there was nothing to fear. That men got excited all the time, that such treatment was standard, and that the gods had much more important things to do. What if she had been wrong?

Psyche suddenly thought of Erik and how wonderful it would have been if she were far from here, protected by his arms, with no fear of a mob that was growing angrier by the minute. But what use was such thought? He was gone. He could not save her. The only person who could save her was herself.

The temple was surprisingly quiet as the guards prevented the mob from entering. Lucius was there to greet them dressed as finely as a priest. His face was stony but his voice held some warmth as he greeted them.

"Psyche, you look well, as always."

Really? Compliments? At such a time? "I feel horrid. Let us get this over with."

His smile vanished, and he grimly led Psyche and her father to the Oracle.

The Oracle was a little man with small eyes and long white hair. His mustache and beard fell as long as his hair. When he raised his eyes, Psyche gasped, for they were a shade of grey so light, they almost matched his irises. Immediately, she got the sense that he was not looking at her, but inside her.

There was no formal introduction, no greeting, no exchange of pleasantries.

"The sacrifice?" He asked.

His voice echoed in the quiet temple.

The sheep was brought in. Psyche could not stop thinking of Erik. Green pastures, smiling shepherd. She gazed sadly at the poor animal. Shadows appeared from behind the Oracle and Psyche realized that there were others waiting in the background, each holding a stick of incense that caused bluish fog to fill the room.

Psyche forced herself to stop trembling and remain still.

"Her hand."

A shadow came from behind. Psyche turned to see the Oracle holding an elaborate knife. Before she could react, he snatched her hand and sliced her palm with the knife, causing Psyche to gasp at the sharp and sudden pain. Then he took the knife stained with her blood and killed the bleating sheep.

The blood fell into a pool creating more smoke and smells that Psyche could not recognize. She felt paralyzed and helpless. The temple was cool and spacious but she suddenly felt as if all the air had left the room and the ceiling was closing in on her. The Oracle chanted in a language she did not recognize. The people behind him chorused the verses, their eyes rolling up as they did so, their voices becoming more and more frenzied. She closed her eyes, not wanting to see their grotesque expressions.

Psyche clutched her hand, willing the stinging to stop. Suddenly, she saw the face of Erik, his smile, and then his frown. Then he was angry with her. And he turned into a sheep. A sheep with horns like sabers. A ram, charging. A Minotaur snarling, chasing after her. As she turned to run, the statue of Aphrodite was suddenly looming right in front her, her beautiful face contorted with snarling rage. The white marble lips opened wide, letting out a piercing, inhuman scream, and blood and snakes began pouring out.

Psyche was on the ground.

She did not remember how she got there.

Psyche's father refused to tell her what the Oracle had discovered. He said he would tell her when they returned home, but his face was ashen. As Psyche passed the angry villagers, she found herself no longer blaming them for their rage. Perhaps they were right. Perhaps she had managed to displease the gods.

When a rotten potato hit her shoulder, she welcomed the pain. She did not know what she had done wrong, but her father's eyes did not lie. She was somehow to blame.

"What is it?" His wife demanded upon seeing them. "Tell me now!"

He did not answer immediately, instead settling himself on a chair, his age finally apparent in his face.

"I would like some warm wine if you could, wife."

"Wine at such a time?"

"Please."

Before she could get the wine, she noticed her daughter's hand. "What did they do?"

"It was just part of the ritual, mother."

When her father was finally settled with his wine before the hearth, he looked at the fire somberly as he spoke.

"The Oracle performed the traditional sacrifice. And when the blood reached the marble floor, he revealed that Psyche's beauty had indeed, offended Olympus. She is to be given, sacrificed, to …a non-mortal. A…a creature of unearthly power. She has no choice but to marry him. It is the only way to lift the curse from the village."

Her sister let out a gasp, and her mother protested vehemently.

"But that is impossible! She has done no wrong. She cannot help being as she is! There must be some mistake."

"There is no mistake," her father's voice was sharp, as if his own grief could only manifest itself in anger. "If we do not do the creature's bidding, a great plague will befall all of us. The whole village will be destroyed."

There was a deathly silence and all turned to Psyche who was the root of all these troubles.

P and T shall live. Be happy.

The irony did not pass her. Death would have been mercy to this.

She thought of the prince she rejected and lost. For whom? For what reason? So that she could be handed to some monster, some beast.

She thought of Erik. And the warm hearth she had always dreamed of with smiling children. Finally the strange man she had always dreamed about had a face. It was Erik's. And it would always be.

Dreams. They couldn't take those away. They couldn't take her memories. She would cherish them, for they may be all she would be allowed to keep.

"We must do what is bidden of us," Psyche murmured.

Without another word, she turned and left the room.

She did not notice that the rain had stopped.

It was the morning before the sacrifice. The conversation with her tearful father the night before still haunted her.

"We can run," he offered, his tormented face moist with tears. "I will take you away from here."

"You must be joking. They will kill mother and Claudia."

"Then we'll take them with us."

Psyche laughed and touched his cheek affectionately. She had thought she had cried the last of her tears, but they flooded her eyes again. "Can you imagine those two on such a journey? We wouldn't make it two paces before they would complain of a blister."

"I cannot bear to think of you..."

"Father, please do not weep. I promise you, things will be all right. You know how I always land on my feet. If I have to make my escape, it will be on my own. By myself. You taught me how to survive. You taught me how to hunt. You are the reason I am as strong as I am. If I am to go down, it will be fighting."

"That does not comfort me."

"I'm sorry. I will send word as soon as I can. Who knows, maybe the creature who will be my husband will enjoy reading as much as I do."

Her father managed a smile.

"You must not fret."

He reached out for her again and they held each other for several minutes.

"What a fool I've been. You are the one being sacrificed and yet it is you comforting me! I do not deserve such a daughter!"

There was no celebration at the house on the seventh hill. There was no excited preparation for a wedding. Instead, her family wore only black.

That morning, Psyche stole away from the house again, armed with her arrows. It could very well be the last day of her life, and she was not going to spend it moping about in her room.

Once she was in the woods, she imagined again taking off, heading towards Pella, escaping her fate. But she knew it would be foolish. The gods would find her, no matter what she did.

It was the first time she had seen the woods since Erik left. She was surprised by how fresh the pain still felt. There was not a trail that did not make her remember him. Every tree seemed to mock her loneliness. She reached the mulberry tree, devoid of berries having been completely picked off by the birds and other small creatures of the woods. She turned away, determined not to mar her last day with intensely depressing thoughts.

Then, she heard a scraping.

Psyche turned and hated herself for hoping. Hoping that Erik would be there, smiling at her as he always seemed to be, in these very woods, waiting to help her out of some distress. She saw a flash of white and strained her eyes.

No, it was not Erik. It was the stag she had seen before when hunting with her father. The wound that her arrow had caused looked to have healed completely.

Psyche notched her arrow. It would be a great prize before her own horrible fate, to bring home a stag for her family. How proud her father would be.

The animal seemed completely unfazed by her. It was offering her an open shot. Still, Psyche did not release the arrow.

Eventually, she lowered her bow and gazed at the animal. It looked up from its leafy meal and returned her look. Its eyes looked almost human, utterly fearless and very wise.

The gods were known to disguise themselves sometimes. Psyche considered the possibility of this stag being one of them. Well, she could use all the help she could get at this point.

She bowed humbly before the animal and said a prayer for her safety and the safety of her family, feeling mildly ridiculous and glad there was no one to see her. But it wouldn't hurt if the lovely animal could tell someone up there, perhaps, that she was not as awful as some might think her to be.

When she looked back up, the stag continued to stand there, looking back at her. Its ears twitched, then it turned and sauntered away.

"Ah, so be it. That was not my first rejection."

Smiling sadly, she turned back towards her home, not noticing the flash of light that burst behind her, streaking straight up to Olympus.

# Acknowledgement

Thank you to my friends and family for giving me so much support and critique without which I would never have finished this book. To Irna Sondang, my amazing editor. To my husband, my Muse. You confirm my belief in love. And for my daughter, my magnum opus now and forever.

A resounding "yawp" to Magistra Jarvis, my High School Latin teacher whose dynamic classes, positive energy, and passion for ancient times inspired a reclusive but impressionable student. For any teacher who wonders if anyone is listening, you'd be surprised just how closely some of us are.

The myth of Eros and Psyche is dear to my heart. The idea that Love could not be complete until it had its Soul struck me as beautiful, powerful, and utterly romantic. Despite contemporary media's portrayal of ancient Greeks as fighters and warriors, let's remember that they were also lovers and philosophers. I have always wanted to share this profound connection between Eros and Psyche to a modern world because I feel like it's still relevant. I truly hope you enjoyed it as much as I enjoyed writing it.

If you liked this first book, please give your feedback and comments. I love reading them, and all new writers need that extra boost. Below, you will find an excerpt to *Book 2 - Scorched*, which should be out soon. Subscribe on my website www.jendelatryst.com or contact me through Twitter and Facebook to get updated as soon as it's available. I would love to hear from you especially if you have any ideas of any female mythological characters that just don't get the recognition they deserve.

Thank you again for choosing my book and lending me your "ears." I will forever be honored and I hope I could borrow them again some time soon.

# Scorched

## Origin of Love Book 2

### Fallen Immortals Saga

## Excerpt

♦

## Jendela Tryst

# Chapter 1

All Psyche could think about was her warm woolen cloak hanging by the hearth she may never see again. She looked down at the edge of the cliff, her red silk garment whipping furiously with the wind, rippling like blood-soaked water. Her beautiful clothes were designed by the most skilled tailor in Pella and elaborately embroidered with pure gold thread. The thin material could not protect her from the chilly gales, but the brown, homespun woolen cloak she longed for would not be appropriate garb for a wedding.

What a farce of a wedding it was. Her family was dressed in black, weeping as if it were her funeral. The priest stood mumbling chants that she could scarcely hear above the howling wind. Psyche peaked again at the edge of the cliff, so very close to her toes.

Would they even care if I simply fell off? Psyche wondered numbly.

Some might have considered it a better fate. Death, at least, was final. Being sacrificed to marry some unknown creature for offending the gods was much more petrifying. Psyche remembered the sheep they had brought to the temple of Aphrodite when they visited the Oracle just a week before. Psyche felt no different than the sheep being led to slaughter with the singing and the ceremony serving only to mask the brutal murder that was about to occur.

The wind died down for a moment, allowing Psyche to hear the priest's shrill voice increasing in volume as he spoke.

"And so, we give to you, Mighty Olympus, this vile offender, who boasted of her beauty as being greater than those of the mighty and sublime Olympians. Who offended, most of all, goddess of beauty, most fair of all goddesses, Aphrodite. May this heathen suffer for her arrogance, her audacity, her unforgiveable blasphemy. May she know true pain and understand the evil of her ways."

For the first time since the announcement of her impending sacrifice, Psyche felt a familiar stir. It was subtle at first, like a distant rainstorm. Then it grew as the priest continued to accuse her. The anger warmed her as if she had gotten her woolen cloak at last.

Anger, however, quickly turned into fury as the priest continued to speak. Psyche had tried to withhold her frustration all week, knowing that there was no way to avoid her fate. Not only would her sacrifice spare the village more death and destruction, but her family's lives were at stake. However, as the priest continued to slice her character with one false accusation after another, blaming her single-handedly for all the misfortunes that the village endured, she felt as if a firebrand had seared her, waking her from her passive trance. She did not realize she had taken a step forward until a guard pressed a spear against her stomach. She could feel the cold sharpness through the flimsy material. The young guard sneered down at her and raised his eyebrows, challenging her to continue.

Without warning, Psyche grabbed the shaft of the spear and angrily pushed it back towards the guard. The combination of Psyche's rage giving her superhuman strength and the element of surprise that she was actually attacking him caused the unsuspecting guard to sprawl back and fall hard on the grassy hill. Two other guards immediately jumped forward and gripped her upper arms. Psyche tried not to wince at the painful force. Within an instant, another spear was back against her stomach.

"Such courageous, strong men!" Psyche taunted, "Fearing an unarmed woman. Perhaps, I will impale you with my silk scarf?"

Psyche's mother Hermena moved forward, but another warning spear held her back.

"Let her go," Hermena cried out. "The child is on edge, she meant no offense! Can you blame the poor thing?"

The priest glared coldly at her mother, then at his enraged captive. He took his time making a decision. His empty gray eyes boldly moved up and down Psyche's form, making her feel instantly repulsed. There was no way to straighten her disheveled gown or hide the skin that had caught the man's indecent attention. The guards held her tightly and the priest knew there was no real threat to him in this party. Only Psyche's mother and her two sisters would defend her, and they were frail little women.

Psyche's father could not attend the ceremony. She was glad of this, for she doubted he would have withstood such words or such treatment of her. When the guards had come to collect Psyche that morning, her father had tried to stop them. Three guards pushed him away with overzealous force. He immediately grew pale and

173

clutched his chest. Psyche helped her mother put him to bed and refused to leave until color returned to his face. Lucius, a village leader and at one time, a friend and previous suitor for Psyche's hand, managed to convince the guards to allow her time to say good-bye to her father in peace.

At least, she could be grateful for that. But not even the sage and well-regarded Lucius could save her from this current humiliation. Her old friend stood not too far behind the priest, a stoic and unfeeling statue, unable or unwilling to help her.

A hot, sweaty finger touched Psyche's face and ran down her neck. She tried to pull away, but the guards held her firmly.

"You have much spirit for a poor farm girl," the priest noted with upturned lip. "No doubt your new husband will enjoy breaking it. But if you try anything like that again, my guards and I will be happy to assist him."

Finally, the priest signaled and the guards slowly released her arms. Immediately, Psyche wrapped her clothes more closely to her, feeling unclean. She forced herself to bite her tongue and stop the angry words she longed to say. Her chance of escape would only come after they left.

The wedding ceremony on the hill proceeded like a dream, but her groom never made his appearance. The mournful wind was the only response to the wedding chant repeated over and over again by the priestesses behind her. Pink flower petals thrown sadly by her sisters soared into the gloomy gray sky.

The priest of Hera, goddess of marriage, sanctified the union and bade Psyche to drink strange nectar in an ornate chalice. It was spicy and sweet but Psyche only took a tiny sip for fear she'd gag. She was supposed to share the drink with her groom, but as he was not present, the chalice was tipped and the brew fell to the ground. Psyche thought the earth swallowed it like a ravenous beast. She shuddered. It must have been her imagination.

Psyche was made to repeat the vows to honor and obey her absent husband and by doing so, honoring and obeying Hera, queen of the gods. The priest reminded her that to try to run or escape her fate would bring dishonor to herself, her family, the village, and to desecrate the name of Hera. It would be the greatest offense to Olympus and a curse would befall all those she loved.

As if she needed more threats.

Psyche tried not to weep when she said good-bye to her family. She didn't want to weep before her enemies and if she started, she didn't think she could ever stop. Instead, she let the cold wind numb her heart again.

Her sisters Elisa and Claudia took turns kissing her cheeks, their lips and tears providing momentary warmth from the frigid air. Just before Psyche thought her quaking legs might fail her, her mother leaned in to say her farewell, her strong hands firm on Psyche's shoulders, her breath mercifully warm against her daughter's cheek. But when Hermena's words registered in Psyche's mind, an icy chill ran down her spine, colder than ever.

"No one can hurt you in the afterlife," her mother murmured. "And no one would blame you. There is no shame if you jump. No shame at all."

When the congregation was gone, Psyche was left alone to fidget by herself on the windy mountaintop. The oracle had said that she must be left alone, for the sight of her groom could send everyone to their deaths. What did that even mean? No one wanted to stay to find out. Psyche knew that the guards were not far. With the cliffs on three sides of her and the guards lining the forest behind her, escape was not very likely.

Her mother was right. There was no other way to run. No one in the village would help her. They blamed her for the plague that devastated the town and the floods that destroyed their land. If she went back to her family, she would put them in danger as well. Besides, where could she run? The gods wanted their sacrifice. And there was no escaping the gods. She did not know what they looked like, but their power was unmistakable, especially after that terrifying visit to the Oracle. Psyche could still remember the bull that charged her and the statue of Aphrodite that screamed at her.

The gods were upset. And the gods were everywhere and knew everything. There was no escape, not with her mortal body weighing her down.

Trembling, Psyche moved towards the edge of the cliff again. She felt her body tingling at the closeness of death. Unable to look down anymore, she moved away

Curse it! She couldn't give up so soon. As long as she still had her wits about her, she could get out of this. Hope leaked into her surprisingly still thriving heart, a slow, vague trickle, but it was there nonetheless. Despite the fact that the gods meant to punish her, despite the fact that Erik, a young man who at one time personified happiness had abandoned her to her tragic fate, and that her family and her village did not want her near them, Psyche could not give up.

She began to pace. There was no escape here, but perhaps her future husband, fearful creature that the oracle claimed he was, would be tolerable. That he might even care for her, for who would go through so much trouble to have her for his wife? Perhaps, he would be easy to outsmart and somehow, some day, she could make her escape.

Yet, as Psyche continued to wait on the cliff, cold and alone, she felt the slim thread of hope slipping farther and farther away. She was waiting to be collected. Like a package, a burden to a groom who did not even bother to show up to their wedding. Care for her? He may even have forgotten about her. And here she was, about to die from the elements. Hope was dying with each gust of cold wind. The Oracle said her groom was a creature. A monster.

Would he devour her right there, just a few miles from her home, leaving her entrails for the villagers to find tomorrow? Or would he take her to his cave somewhere and enjoy her slowly piece by piece?

Psyche shuddered. No, she could not allow it to happen!

Psyche looked towards the forest where she knew guards stood watch beyond the plateau. On three sides of her, the ground jutted down. She scanned the sharp drop and got dizzy at the plunging view beneath her. There had to be a way to escape! The guards couldn't wait forever. Perhaps, if she hid somewhere, they would think she had been collected, or committed suicide, and would go on their way.

But there was nowhere to hide. Not unless she could cling to the edge of the cliff.

Realizing that it was a possibility, Psyche began walking around the perimeter of the plateau with renewed hope. All she could see were smooth rock and loose limestone. Psyche rubbed her hands together. She had to survive. She couldn't just let some creature take her, or let herself die of the freezing cold.

Finally, she spotted it. At the left edge of the cliff, she saw a jutting ledge that might withstand her weight. It was just far down enough that anyone who looked would not be able to see her. If she gathered some grass and dropped it down, she might be able to hide under it. But she did not have rope, and she did not know if she would be able to get back up again if she did manage to get on the ridge. There was no point in going down if she could not climb back up. She would die before sunrise from the freezing wind.

Looking around, Psyche spied some fallen branches near the forest. Perhaps, she could make a crude ladder? She approached the trees cautiously. A guard suddenly appeared, then another. They stood with their hands on their spears, a grim and intimidating line, looking cold and detached back at her.

Psyche backed away and returned to her clearing, trying not to let the panic overwhelm her. Something caught her foot and she fell forward. Tears streamed down her face as she clutched her ankles. Then she saw what it was she had tripped on. It was a rock. Psyche picked one up as an idea formed in her mind. She could gather some rocks and hammer them into the dirt to create footholds. It was a slim chance, but at least it was a chance.

Shaking with anticipation, Psyche returned to the edge of the cliff where a small slope blocked the guards' view of her. She began collecting sharp stones and carried them to the edge of the cliff just above the ledge. She let the stones fall until several landed on the ridge. After that, she tore armfuls of grass and also dropped them. All she needed to do now was lower herself and wait for nightfall. The ledge was almost twice her height beneath her. She would need to drop slowly, so as not to stumble back and fall headfirst over the cliff. Her hands were still numb with cold and difficult to trust. She needed to warm them before she attempted such a climb.

Psyche began jumping in place while blowing into her cupped palms. She needed to think of something warm. Something that could make her angry again. Her thoughts wandered to a young shepherd named Erik, who had once been the center of her world. Was it only a few weeks ago that she waited for him to meet her on a lonely hill, very similar to this one? How different life had been then. The toughest decision she had was whether to marry the charming, wealthy, if a little dull Prince Lagan, or run away with the poor, illiterate, but devastatingly charming shepherd, Erik. Psyche was a different person then. And when Erik abandoned her, never to be seen again, her spirit ran off with him. Where was Erik now, she wondered? Perhaps the rumors were true, that he was merely a charlatan, a womanizer who moved from town to town to sate his lusts. But how could lust be his motive when she had offered herself to him and he refused, saying that only a marriage bed would satisfy him.

Psyche blushed when she remembered how shamelessly she had acted. But, he stopped her. Why? It was not the act of a charlatan. Perhaps, all he really wanted was her heart. Perhaps, all he wanted was the chase. Perhaps he was already married to someone else. Perhaps all of it was just lies.

There was no end to the possibilities when it came to the mysterious disappearance of Erik. He left her a single note and nothing more. Psyche blinked back the angry tears that were threatening to unravel her. At least the pain and hot resentment she felt when she thought of Erik served its purpose. She felt warm and angry all over.

She would not let them win. Not Erik, not the priest, not even Aphrodite.

Psyche crept to the edge and looked again at the ledge that was now her only refuge. Rubbing her hands together, she tested the tall weeds that fell over the cliff like an unruly fringe. They were surprisingly sturdy. Taking a deep breath, she sat down with her legs dangling perilously over the cliff. Her heart jumped violently in her chest, making it hard for her to breathe.

Swallowing hard, Psyche turned onto her stomach and wrapped the thick grass around her wrists and grasped firmly.

Saying a quiet prayer to whatever gods still held her in favor, she began to lower herself bit by bit. She could not see where the ledge was, but she estimated that it wouldn't be too far from her feet. Psyche continued to let herself sink slowly down, trying to get as low as possible. Her shoulders shook with the effort, but she bid herself to continue her slow descent. There was no point in escaping if she had a broken leg.

Right when she was certain her arms would give way, she heard a voice. For a moment, she thought it was the wind playing tricks on her. The rumble of her stomach perhaps, from hunger. She should have drunk more of that sweet drink offered by the priest.

The sound came again, forming words so clear, she found herself looking around for the source. Had someone come to check on her?

"Father?" she called out.

She could see no one.

"Mother?"

Again, there was only the baleful wind. Psyche could not see much, but she was certain the voice was coming from behind her where nothing but grey sky loomed. Psyche's arms were starting to ache, the grass wrapped around her wrist cutting off her blood flow. Still, she held on tightly and somehow, the weeds continued to hold her weight.

A cold thought entered her mind. Was she finally being collected?

Her already pounding heart began to beat even more furiously. How could she escape from a winged harpy, a two-headed dragon, or a rock golem waiting to devour her?

Another frantic look around revealed nothing except thick fog. The only change was that the wind seemed to slightly increase in speed.

Finally, Psyche thought she deciphered a phrase.

"Let go?" she repeated out loud.

What prankster was this? But the voice came again, and Psyche really did start to wonder if she was going mad. Then she heard a sickening crunching sound. The weeds her hands were gripping were starting to tear apart. There was nowhere to run, nowhere to go. Except down.

"No!" she cried out. "I want to live!"

She struggled to climb back up and get away from the strange voice that was clouding her mind.

"You will not die," assured the voice. "I shall catch you. Never fear."

Now these were words that she could not have made up, and she suddenly realized that it was the wind that was speaking to her. It was circling and circling in such a way that made her feel suddenly lightheaded. Her hair whipped around her, momentarily blocking her sight. The cool, whipping air dried the tears that had been streaming down her face. She did not even realize that she had been crying. Psyche was being pulled, not down, towards the ledge, but farther out towards the bleak, gray sky.

She gasped and tried to struggle from the invisible force that was pulling her back. She clawed at the edge, grabbing onto more grass, all of which ripped from her fingers.

She was not ready for her death.

"I cannot! Please, don't!"

This time, the wind was more insistent and Psyche found herself slipping even as her nails dug frantically deep into the dirt. "No.... Please!" But there was nothing more to grab. She made a feeble attempt to grasp the ledge that had once provided so much hope, but it only struck her fingers, causing a sharp pain.

She screamed. And then she was falling.

CPSIA information can be obtained
at www.ICGtesting.com
Printed in the USA
LVHW102135260722
724509LV00018B/464